Relationships
& Iden.

Elizabeth Lutzeier was born in Manchester and has
lived in Berlin, California and the East End of London
before moving to her current job as head teacher of
a large comprehensive school. She won the Kathleen
Fidler Award in 1984 for her first novel, *No Shelter*.

Other books by Elizabeth Lutzeier

No Shelter
The Coldest Winter
The Wall
Bound for America

Lost for Words

Elizabeth Lutzeier

MACMILLAN CHILDREN'S BOOKS

First published 1993 by Oxford University Press

First published 1996 by Macmillan Children's Books
This edition published 2001 by Macmillan Children's Books
a division of Macmillan Publishers Limited
20 New Wharf Road, London N1 9RR
Basingstoke and Oxford
www.panmacmillan.com

Associated companies throughout the world

ISBN 0 330 39820 2

3 5 7 9 8 6 4 2

A CIP catalogue record for this book is available from the British Library.

Phototypeset by Intype London Ltd
Printed and bound in Great Britain by Mackays of Chatham plc, Kent

There are many people I need to thank for helping me to write this story. I want to thank my colleagues at Plashet School, who believed in the future for pupils like Aysha. I need to thank Ratna Ambett, Janet Roberton, and Marco Johnston from Newham's INSEC, who gave me so much support and encouragement while I was writing.

But most of all, this book is my way of saying thank you to Aysha and Fateha, Supriya and Ferdous, Happirun and Shamima, Severa and Parveen. Because this is their story.

Chapter One

'There's a foreigner coming! I can see a foreigner!'

Aysha was always the first one to climb to the top of one of the palm trees, like a row of street lamps, that lined the track leading away from her grandfather's land. She was always the first to the end of the track when they raced each other from Dada's land to their nearest neighbour's house. And out of all Dada's grandchildren, she was always the first to wrestle a ball from one of her uncles and run fast with the ball all the way to her grandfather, while he stood and watched and laughed in the door of his house. Aysha was stronger and faster and more agile than any of her cousins. But when she saw the cart on the horizon she stopped short of the top of the tree. It was Husain who called out.

'I know it's a foreigner. I can tell a foreigner from a hundred fields away.'

The warm rain of the monsoon swished a gentle chorus to the words that Husain sang out. But Aysha, with a rice sack round her shoulders, kept quiet and made her way slowly down the tree. She knew who was coming.

Then Komla huddled next to Aysha under one of the bamboo shelters in Dada's plantation. From high up above them, right at the top of the coconut palm, Husain sang out again. 'It's a real foreigner! A man

1

in a suit. He's riding on Jamiluddin's ox cart. Look! He's got an umbrella with all the rainbow colours on it.'

'That's not a foreigner.'

Aysha let the rice sack drop on the floor of the shelter and ran out into the rain. In a second she could hardly open her eyes for the little rivers of rain that cascaded down from her short hair. She wanted to run away, far away from Dada's house and yard and the plantation with its tall coconut palms and mango trees. But during the rainy season her grandfather's compound was an island. All his fields were covered with water. And the only way out was the raised up road lined with palm trees, the road that was bringing Jamiluddin's ox cart nearer all the time they spoke.

'Aysha! You're not supposed to climb the trees. Your mother said so. You're not to go near that tree again!'

Komla peeped out from under the bamboo shelter and then pulled her head back in again. Like Aysha, she had glistening, wet hair, as short as most of the boys. Shaving their heads kept the lice away in the hot weather and by the time the rains came their shaved heads had grown glossy, short, dark hair again. Both the girls wore gold earrings.

Husain wasn't supposed to climb trees, either. During the rainy season two years before, he had climbed to the top of a palm tree right on the edge of Dada's land overhanging the river – because he said he wanted to see what the people in India were doing. When he fell out of the tree and into the water, his cousins had laughed. Husain was a good swimmer.

But Aysha had had to pull him out and his leg was broken. Then Dada had paid the Hindu doctor to mend his leg – hundreds of taka, everyone said. But Husain still walked with a limp. Husain's Ama said it was because Dada had asked a Hindu doctor to set the leg. Their grandmother said it was because there was an Indian ghost living in the river who took away the lives of the people of Bangladesh, inch by inch. Dada told his wife she was a silly old woman.

Aysha didn't need to climb right to the top of the tree any more. She could see the bright umbrella, like a sail carrying Jamiluddin's ox cart through the flooded fields, when she was only halfway up the tree. But they couldn't see any faces. Jamiluddin, as usual, had his back bent forward as if someone had beaten him with a hundred lashes the night before. The oxen shimmered like mother of pearl in the mist and rain but they kept their heads down. And the bright umbrella covered the face that Aysha dreaded.

'Iqbal's got a ball to play with!' she shouted as she shinned down the tree. 'They're playing behind Mofi's house.'

'But what about the foreigner?'

'They're still half an hour away. Waiting for Jamiluddin's cart is like watching for the rice to grow.'

'We could go to meet them.' Husain began to climb down the tree, much more slowly than Aysha.

Aysha ran off through the rain, leaping over ripe mangoes brought down in the storm of the night before. 'I'm going to play with the ball.'

Komla chased after her, clutching the corners of the rice sack over her head and Husain was left alone to walk out through the back of the yard on to the

3

narrow road. From outside the gate to his grand-father's compound, Jamiluddin's cart wasn't even a gnat-sized speck on the horizon. He went back in and limped over to the yard behind Mofi's house where the girls had joined the rest of his cousins, kicking a ball in a wild game of football in the rain.

'There's a foreigner coming,' Husain said.

Iqbal, at thirteen and a half, was the oldest of all the grandchildren. 'There's no foreigners come here in the rainy season,' he said. 'Who would want to come to Jamdher?'

Aysha pulled a face. She knew who was coming. She knew she should go and tell her mother, go and tell her grandmother to cook the rice. They had been waiting and watching the road for weeks, waiting for news and watching for signs of the visitor from England.

Aysha was surprised at how easily her cousins had forgotten. Only a week before, Dada had pronounced that the visitor would not come now that the rains had set in. And whenever her grandfather made a pronouncement, no one dared to argue with him. Dada had said that no foreign visitor would bother trying to get through to Jamdher once the monsoon had started and Iqbal believed him. But Aysha had seen the ox cart and the brightly coloured umbrella and she knew they were getting closer. She picked up the ball and ran with it, furious and fast, so that the others chased after her, whooping and laughing and tripping up in the huge puddles of rainwater.

Mofi's Ama pulled aside the damp curtain in front of their door and Aysha saw her mother and grand-mother standing there, laughing as the children fell around in the warm rain. Dadi, her grandmother, shouted, 'Watch out, Aysha! They're after you,' and she was suddenly brought down in the deepest puddle in Mofi's yard. She pulled a face at her grandmother and laughed and jumped up again, chasing Iqbal with the ball. The rainy season, when the waters were too high for them to go to school and they all sat round and did their reading with their grandmother, and all learned and played together every day, was the best time, the warmest time of the year.

Aysha ignored the man in the suit. He came through into the yard with one arm round Dada's shoulders and the other still clutching the huge, bright umbrella. One by one, as they noticed the visitor, the children stopped playing and walked shyly across the yard to stand near him and inspect his clothes. Soon only Aysha was left, struggling to get the ball from Iqbal, fighting to ignore the man she didn't want to see.

'She won't give up,' laughed Dada. 'She's a fighter. One day she'll be a Prime Minister, like Indira Ghandi or Benazir Bhutto. She's going to be a great woman, my granddaughter. You'll see.'

The man with the umbrella stood there in Mofi's doorway. 'I still don't know which one she is,' he said. 'They all look like boys to me. And all of them strange. In five years, how much has changed.' He patted Mofi on the head and turned to Aysha's grandmother. 'This can't be Mofi, the baby that was never meant to live?'

Dadi smiled. 'You've lost count. You've been away more than five years. It's nearly six years since you last came home to us. Mofi had to fight to live.' Her face was a kaleidoscope of smiles. 'Aysha would never have lived either, if Dada hadn't been sick, too, when she was a baby and taken the time to feed her every hour because he was lying in bed with nothing better to do. She's always been his favourite.'

'But which one is Aysha? Aysha!' the man called. He turned to Aysha's mother, who stood in the background, behind Dadi. 'You should dress my daughter like a woman,' he said. 'Not like one of the boys, rolling in the dirt.'

Dada scolded him. 'She's still a child,' he said. 'I want my granddaughter to have time to be a child. She's barely thirteen. There'll be time enough for her to be a woman.' Then he clapped his hands. Aysha and Iqbal stopped squabbling over the ball and stood before him, the rain streaming from their faces. Iqbal grinned at the stranger, but Aysha looked down at the ground.

Aysha's mother took the edge of her sari and wiped her daughter's eyes.

'You're not shy in front of your father, are you?'

Then everybody laughed and Dada pulled Aysha close to him. 'I never thought I would see the day when Aysha had nothing to say. Just wait,' he said to Aysha's father, 'no one ever gets the chance to talk when Aysha's around. You'll soon be cracking your sides with laughter, the things she says.'

The stranger, Aysha's father, looked at his daughter and stroked and held out ribbons of her wet hair as if he were examining an animal he was thinking of buying from a pet shop.

'She's very small for her age, isn't she?'

Chapter Two

The weeks passed and the monsoon rains gradually gave way to occasional violent thunderstorms. Aysha's hair grew long enough to plait into two short braids which stuck out at the side of her head. She got used to calling the stranger from England Aba, father – at first because Dadi scolded her until she used the strange word, but then, slowly, because she was proud that she, too, had a father, like all her other cousins.

It wasn't long before her father stopped wearing his stiff, grey English suit and began to look more like Aysha's uncles in his lunghi and vest. And when the rice harvest came, he was out in the fields with her uncles and Dada and the hired labourers. She began to think that this time he had come to stay.

Aysha's father still spoke in a strange way, so that the other children in Jamdher called him the English Man and stared at him whenever he went past. But slowly, as the weeks went by, the man who had existed only in the letters her mother couldn't read and the English money, which her mother always gave straight to Dada, became a living person.

All the same, Aysha still thought of Dada as her real father. Of all his grandchildren, she knew that she was his favourite. She alone, of all the grandchildren, had lived in her grandfather's large, concrete house with the sturdy tin roof since she was born. It was not that Aysha's uncles were poor. They all had good, corrugated metal roofs over their houses, too, but the walls of their houses were made of bamboo.

It was in Dada's house that the Eid festivals were always celebrated. And the beggar women, carrying all their gossip and all their ghost stories from village to village, stopped in her grandmother's kitchen, not at any of the six smaller houses scattered all around, belonging to her father's six brothers. In Dadi's kitchen, the beggar women wandering through Jamdher emptied out all their stories on to her bamboo woven floor in exchange for the rice which Aysha's mother measured out for them, while Aunt Piara made some tea and Dadi sat and listened.

Aysha's grandfather would never deny her anything. No one had ever heard him shouting at her as he sometimes shouted at her cousins. So when her father arrived, Dada soon made it clear to him, too, that Aysha was not to be scolded.

'She's a good girl when she has to be,' he said. 'She helps her grandmother when they need help in the kitchen. But Piara is there too. There are enough women. Let Aysha be a child. She'll be a woman soon enough.'

Dadi told visitors proudly that her son was a factory manager in London. Aysha remembered how often her grandmother had read his letters out to every beggar woman who came by. And she liked to show them the English money he sent, so that Dada had to scold her.

'Do you want thieves to come and visit us in the night?' he said.

Aysha's mother never said anything when Dadi showed the letters to everyone who came to their house. It wasn't right for her to argue with her husband's mother, and anyway, she couldn't read. She needed her mother-in-law to read the letters. After Aysha had learned to read, she offered to read her father's letters aloud to her mother.

'Dadi doesn't have to see them,' she said. 'The letters are for you and me.'

But her mother was shocked. 'Aba is her son,' she said. 'You should be grateful to Dadi for teaching you to read. She said she's going to make Dada pay for you to go to High School. You can't keep Aba's letters secret from her.'

After Dada had spoken to him, Aysha's father stopped shouting at her for playing outside with the other children instead of doing the housework. But he was still a foreigner, still different to her uncles. He never had time to sit and listen to stories while the women did the cooking. He was impatient. Through the bamboo wall, Aysha heard him talking to her uncle about the time he was wasting, going to market once a week, waiting and waiting for the harvest or the right time to weed the rice seedlings. He hadn't meant to stay so long in Jamdher, he said. He had important business to attend to in London.

Aysha gradually realized that the main reason for her father's visit was not to see her and her mother but to attend the wedding. Aunt Piara was his only sister. She had waited a long time. Some people said she was too choosy. But finally she was going to be married to the son of Kamal, a local landowner. And

9

Aysha's father couldn't understand why the wedding had not been arranged before he arrived. Dada grumbled at him.

'You are too English. You think you can control everything. But what about Allah? Only Allah decides when the time is right for Piara to be married. And it has to be the best of weddings for my only daughter. It takes time.'

Aba didn't have time. He was the only person who wore a watch and that meant he didn't have any time. He kept saying he had important business to attend to in London. But there was something else he wouldn't say. Something was wrong. A week before the wedding, he went away again in Jamiluddin's ox cart. Aysha's mother didn't know where he had gone and Dada wouldn't say. All the children said he must have gone to Dhaka, because he wore his English suit.

Two days before the wedding he was back again, arriving this time in a whirlwind of dust that turned out to be a taxi followed by all the children who had managed to run behind it on the narrow, bumpy causeway of a road raised up between the fields. Something was wrong.

'What's the matter, Dadi?'

Aysha's grandmother swatted impatiently at the swarm of flies that dared to hover over the mountain of fresh chicken she was cutting into smaller pieces. Supriya, the wife of one of the labourers who always helped Dada with the harvest, was grinding a mix of spices in a huge bowl, covering herself with yellow turmeric.

'Nothing. Nothing's the matter, you silly child. Go and help your mother.'

Aysha's mother looked hot and tired, stirring Dadi's largest pot full of dhal.

'What's the matter, Ama?'

Ama was wearing her fourth-best sari, the white one with a blue border. She pushed her hair back with the back of her hand.

'Nothing's the matter. What should be the matter? Your aunt is going to be married. We have enough to do without your silly questions. Go and help your grandmother.'

'Dadi told me to come and help you. But something's the matter.'

'I have enough to do without finding work for you. Nothing's wrong. Now go and play.'

Aysha didn't feel like playing, joining her cousins who were climbing over the taxi while the driver smoked a cigarette with her father and grandfather in the yard. She pushed her way under the washing on the lines in the yard, hoping to cool off by brushing against the damp cotton of her mother's best sari. But the washing she had helped to hang up only ten minutes before was already dry.

Something was wrong. Aunt Piara was going to be married in two days and she would be leaving home to live in her husband's house. But Kamal's land and the place where his son had started to build a house for Piara was next to Dada's house in Jamdher. She would be able to visit whenever she wanted. So that wasn't why they were all so sad, so angry.

There had never been a wedding in Dada's house before, but Aysha could remember other great parties and Eid festivals and the way Dadi had always enjoyed bossing everyone around in her kitchen, always making sure the most delicious food was served. But now Dadi was angry. Something was wrong.

The thin cotton saris and lunghis on the line hung like quiet, tired old men. Aysha buried her head in the cloth of her grandmother's deep blue sari and then peeped out at each one of her aunts as they ran backwards and forwards across the courtyard with steaming hot dishes of rice or dhal or fish. Then she went to look for her grandfather. The taxi driver had gone and her father was nowhere to be seen. Her grandfather was sitting on a stool outside the kitchen door, smoking a cigarette.

'What's the matter, Dada?'

Dada coughed for a long time before he could answer her. He wasn't used to smoking real cigarettes, like the ones her father had brought from England for the wedding. Dadi rushed out of the kitchen, grabbed the cigarette out of his mouth and threw it far away from them and into the fire.

'Those English cigarettes will kill you, you silly old man,' she said. She stood for a moment out in the yard, twisting her long, grey hair round and round until it tied itself into a knot on the back of her head. Dada winked at Aysha. 'Nobody wants us,' he said. 'Your father took them all off with the taxi to the market in town. The boys went too. There's only Komla left.'

'She's helping her mother,' Aysha said.

'Yes. She's a good girl.' Dada smiled. He took hold of Aysha's wrist and pushed himself up from the step.

12

'You've helped your mother already, haven't you? Let's get away from here. Nobody wants us.' He put his arm through Aysha's and turned away from the yard and the noise of the wedding preparations. 'You are going to go to college, aren't you, Aysha?'

Some of the other men in Jamdher, even Kamal, who had sent his son to college, said it was a waste to educate a girl. But Dada was different. He liked it when Aysha's grandmother read to him at night. He said there was no harm in teaching a woman how to read. And then he used to say that if she could read she might as well do a good job. Dada was different to the other men in Jamdher because he had seen the world. He had even been to England when he was young.

'Husain may go to college,' he said, 'but you're the really clever one.' He winked. 'The teacher told me.'

They walked over towards the plantation. Dada said he wanted to talk to his jackfruit tree. 'There's a fruit on there, bigger than a man's head. I want to be sure it's right for Piara's wedding.'

Aysha held her grandfather's hand. 'What's the matter, Dada?'

'You're the clever one,' he said. 'You're the one who's going to be something in this family.' He reached up and touched the spiky, hard skin of the jackfruit, patting it gently as if it were an animal. 'A lot of people say girls don't need to go to college. Your father thinks like that. But your Dadi can read and it didn't do her any harm. It didn't stop me wanting to marry her. And Piara went to High School and look what a good husband she will have. It's a fine thing, when a woman has education.'

13

Aysha waited and listened. She wanted to ask again, 'What's the matter?' But she didn't repeat her question. Dada always gave her an answer, in a roundabout way. She knew he would tell her what her mother and grandmother were keeping from her. If he knew what was wrong, he would tell her.

'I can send you to High School, Aysha. For a year or two. But it's expensive, and who knows how long I've still got to live?'

Aysha squeezed her grandfather's thin hand. 'I'll look after you, Dada. You're never going to die. Not while I'm here.'

'Aysha, your father is going to take you to live in England with him. You and your mother.'

Aysha smiled at her grandfather. He had never forced her to do anything she didn't want to do. She knew he never would.

'Let me stay with you, Dada,' she said. 'I don't want to go to England.'

But her grandfather had no answer. He hunched his shoulders as if he felt cold. Then he sat down, slumped against the jackfruit tree, looking very small. 'I don't know what to do. It's what your father wants. He has a good job in England.'

Aysha stood in front of him, her hands on her hips. 'But why can't he stay here? Like my uncles. He could work with you. There's enough here for everyone. We don't need to go to England.'

Dada shook his head. 'You don't want him to be poor, do you? Do you want him and your uncles to end up with no land, like Ruhul Amin and his family?'

Aysha frowned. 'But you have land, Dada. We're not like Ruhul's family. They're poor.'

'Husain's mother is having twins. And Piara will take her share of the land to her husband when I die. There won't be enough to feed you all. It's good if your father can earn money with his work in England.'

Aysha kicked at the soft, damp ground, burying her feet in the mound of leaves around the tree. 'Well, he can go then. Let him go there and earn his money. I'm not going to England. I have to stay here and look after you and Dadi. He's all right on his own. And he can always come to visit us again.'

That night, Aysha fell asleep to the sound of frogs singing, the sound of crickets chirping, and the soft sound of her mother crying in the next room.

The sound which woke her was a shrill crying she had never heard before, and there were suddenly lights being lit all over the compound. Her mother shouted, 'A snake! Aysha, lie still! A snake!'

But there was no snake in Aysha's room. Only one of the frogs that sometimes hopped in and out through the bamboo screen. Dada came in with his kerosene lamp, searching in every corner of her room and the frog hopped away. Once again, they heard the strange, shrill scream and Dada put his arm around Aysha. 'Don't worry,' he said. 'The snake has caught another frog. We'll catch the snake too, if he doesn't go away.' But there were no more sounds that night.

'We haven't had a snake so close to the house for years,' Dadi said, as she combed Aysha's hair next morning. 'Someone's brought evil spirits out of the jungle. If a snake steals a frog it means a spirit's going to take a child away.' Aysha's grandmother knew there were evil spirits around because she'd seen them with her own eyes. And while she twisted Aysha's hair into two short plaits, Dadi told her the story she'd heard many times before, how Dadi had been sitting talking late at night with Husain's mother when a man walked through the wall.

'It was in Dada's house. This very house,' Aysha's grandmother said. 'Now you just touch that hard, concrete wall and tell me how a living man could walk through walls like that, if you can. But the man did walk through them, straight through the outside wall. He must have been a spirit.' She smoothed some oil on Aysha's hair, so that it shone. 'The spirit man said that Husain was his, that he was going to take the child before he was four years old.' Dadi's mouth became fixed and stern. 'But we didn't let him. We kept Husain inside the house and watched over him night and day until he was five years old and the danger was past.' She nodded. 'That's how clever you have to be when there's spirits around.' She smiled. 'And the spirit was so angry when we beat him that he took a bite out of Husain's leg last year, when he made Husain fall out of that tree and break his leg. He won't be able to take Husain away from us now, but he'll still be angry. I've always watched over you, Aysha, over all my children and my grandchildren. And I always will. I won't let the spirits harm you.'

Aysha felt sick. She hardly noticed the three days of wedding celebrations. Her grandfather had paid for a man from Sylhet to come with a video camera and film everything that happened. Later everyone said how strange it was that Aysha only appeared once on the film. It was as if she didn't belong to the family any more, as if she were one of the beggar children who always hung around, peeping in at the door when they were celebrating, waiting for someone to throw them some scraps to eat. She wanted Dada to do something, to insist that his granddaughter was going to stay in Jamdher with him. She wanted him to say that he wouldn't let her go to England. Otherwise, it was as if her grandfather had sent her away. And if her grandfather didn't do anything to keep her there, if he didn't shout at her father and forbid him to take her away, what right did she have, after all, to feel she belonged?

Piara, the bride, sat with her eyes cast down whenever the man with his camera was there, filming the women as they decorated her hands with mehndi patterns or all trooped down to the pond to collect water. But as soon as the women were left alone, she teased Aysha.

'What has your father done to you now? I've never known you to be so quiet.'

Aysha said nothing. It was all right for Piara. She was only moving to a house at the far side of Dada's land. Dadi would cry because she cried at every marriage ceremony and because Piara was her only daughter and her youngest child. It was normal for people to cry at a wedding. But Aysha watched her mother's face, where she sat in the shadows behind Piara. Two deep furrows had been channelled in her face by tears. Nobody had asked Ama what she wanted to do.

'I wish I was going to England,' said Piara. She looked so beautiful in her red sari embroidered with

17

gold. She looked so different to the Piara who worked hard with the other women, weaving bamboo baskets and mats and embroidering caps. She was always so busy, just like Dadi, so restless and eager to work. Now she sat very, very still while the women arranged her hair and made her face magical with make-up.

Aysha, in her red dress, her hair tightly plaited, kept her face as miserable as she felt and didn't say a word.

'Have you ever known Aysha to keep quiet?' Aunt Piara laughed. 'You're not the one who's supposed to be sad. I'm the one who's leaving my mother and father.' She slapped Aysha's cheek gently three times. 'Hey! You're the cleverest one. Dada says so.'

Dadi interrupted, smiling and nodding proudly, 'None of my other grandchildren could read so quickly.'

'Listen! Aysha!' Piara shook her by the elbow, but Aysha turned away. The special wedding patterns traced on the floor swam round and round in front of her and she felt sick. 'You're a silly girl,' Piara said. 'In England, your father has a fine house. And you'll be able to go to college. Perhaps you'll be a secretary for the government in Dhaka.' Her make-up was finally finished and the women all around her gasped as they saw how beautiful she looked. Piara had never had make-up on before.

'Just imagine how proud Dada will be when you go to college. We'll all be so proud of you, Aysha. Just imagine what an honour that would be for our family. When you go to England, Aysha, you can do so much for your family, if you work hard at school.

That's what you mustn't forget. You're not leaving us. You're taking our family out into the world.'

Aysha and her mother had never left Jamdher before. They had never been to Sylhet, with its rush of rickshaw drivers weaving their way in between lorries and buses and ox carts and jeeps. They had never been on a train until they made the twelve hour train journey to Dhaka. And Aysha had only ever seen an aeroplane thousands of feet away up in the sky until they started to board their plane for London at Dhaka International Airport.

It might have been different. If they had known they were coming back to Jamdher, Aysha would have been thrilled at the chance to ride in the red-painted rickshaw cab with a picture of Prince Charles and Princess Diana on the back and with long red and gold fringes round the outside. But she sat next to her mother and held her hand while Ama stared at the world outside as if she were a child scared of going to sleep in case she had a nightmare. If the train had been only a holiday trip, Aysha would have played games with her father, counting the rivers they had to cross or the travelling people in boats they saw from the windows. But her father looked stern and impatient and kept looking at his English watch. In his grey, English suit, he didn't look like Aba any more. And the train's wheels drummed out Husain's words again and again.

'There's a foreigner here. There's a foreigner here.'

If the plane had been taking them to England for a few weeks, just to see where Aysha's father lived, so that they could have a picture in their minds when his letters came, Aysha would have jumped at the chance to tell the others in her class at school all about the air hostesses greeting everyone like royalty and the dainty food on little dishes and the special armchair seats.

But they were leaving Bangladesh for ever. All the time he had stayed in Jamdher, Aysha's father had never missed the chance of telling all the visitors who came to see him how much his fare had cost from England and how he had had to save to come home for five years. And everyone had gasped with horror because the money he had paid would have fed a poor man and his family for more than a year. And everyone patted Aysha's father on the back and said, 'It's a good thing you could get the money, eh? A good thing you're not poor.' If he had to save up that money for three people, it could take fifteen years before they saw their country again.

They were leaving Bangladesh for ever. And Aysha's father kept on looking at his English watch. He couldn't wait to be back in England. For the first time since they had left the village he smiled as the plane took off.

'Now you'll see something,' he said. 'Take a look out of that window.' Ama covered her face with her veil and cried. And there were other women on the plane like her, shutting themselves off from the world.

Aysha leaned across her mother, to look out of the round window and back towards land. At first she could only see green, the emerald green of Bangladesh's lush, fertile fields, threaded with silver rivers and streams. Then she gasped. Over to the west the sun was a disc of crimson gold just about to set.

Bangladesh had become a land of gold. Quickly she looked over to the other window. The plane had tilted upwards, gaining height. And the sky was already grey and cold.

Chapter Three

Aysha had never seen grey shoes before. She had seen black shoes made khaki or green with dust and mould and rain. But she had never seen shiny, grey shoes and she didn't like them. Everything in England was grey and shiny. The floor at the airport shone with mottled, marbled grey lino. Their suitcases were unpacked and then everything thrown back in again by a woman with a grey face. And a man in a grey suit with shiny grey shoes came to meet them at the airport in a car with rusty dents and scratches breaking up its shiny, grey surface.

His name was Faruk and he said he came from Sylhet. But Aysha didn't believe him. He spoke too much like an Englishman, almost as if he had had to learn Bengali at school and had never been very good at it. Aysha's father said, 'Faruk's going to take us to our landlord's house. It's very good of him to come out all this way to pick us up.'

Aysha was tired and angry. She wanted to say, 'Dadi tells everyone you have your own house in London. We thought you were very rich.' But Aba spoke first. 'Faruk knows I'm only renting for a short time – until we can buy a house. Everyone buys houses in England.'

It was raining. Aba took a deep breath and said,

'It's good to be out of that plane and into the fresh air.' Then he lit a cigarette.

Faruk took one of Aba's cigarettes and drew at it before he picked up Aysha's suitcase. 'It's a pity it's raining,' he said.

'We're used to rain,' Aysha's father said. 'We've had plenty of rain in Jamdher. You wouldn't believe how much rain! That's why we're two weeks later than I thought. We couldn't get through to Dhaka, the rain was that bad. But we don't mind a bit of rain, do we, Aysha?'

Aysha didn't want to open her mouth. She didn't want to breathe. When the rains came in Jamdher, the air was always fresher and cleaner while the roads waded deeper in dirt. In London, in the dark car park outside the airport, the roads glistened as if someone had been polishing them, while the air smelt of dirt and evil, choking smoke, and tar. She caught hold of her mother's hand and they sat quietly, holding hands, for the whole of the bumpy ride to an unknown house in the unknown city.

Aysha felt sick and weary and ready to sleep, but through her half-sleep she still listened to her father arguing with Faruk.

'This isn't the right way. You could have gone down the Commercial Road.'

'I know where I'm going.'

'You're the driver. But I just think the other way would have been better.'

Faruk gritted his teeth. 'I know where I'm going. Look, I'm doing you a favour.'

Faruk was much younger than Aysha's father. She had only once heard a young man speaking like that to someone older than him, and that was when Kamal the landowner's son had shouted at one of their labourers.

'But now we've driven past it,' said Aysha's father.

Faruk pulled over to the left side of the road. It was very early in the morning and the roads were almost empty. Every so often, an empty bus raced through the darkness, spraying Faruk's car with water. A few other cars hissed past on the other side of the road.

'Look. I'm doing you a big favour,' Faruk said. 'Because we are both Muslim brothers and Bangladeshis. I don't have to do this, but I couldn't leave you with nowhere to go to with your wife and daughter.' His jaws worked hard at a piece of chewing gum while he thought about what to say next. 'I would have written to you, but you know how letters never get through.'

'I know you don't like writing.' Aysha's father was immediately very angry and she couldn't tell why. She thought he was going to start hitting Faruk. Her mother shivered and pulled her sari round her tightly and clung to Aysha's arm, but nothing could keep out the chill September air.

'Your landlord's let the house again,' said Faruk. The road was empty and all they heard was the swish of rain on the windscreen. Faruk pulled at the chewing gum stuck between his bottom front teeth. 'Look, you can have a room in one of my houses for a week. Until you find somewhere.'

'I paid my rent. He can't do that. I thought there were laws in England. If you pay your rent, they can't turn you out.'

Ama shrank back into her corner at the back of the car, as if she wanted to be still asleep, to close her eyes and wake up home again. Aba was bitter and angry and out of breath from shouting.

Faruk leaned across Aysha's father and opened the passenger door. 'If you don't pay your rent, he doesn't have to give you a house free of charge. And if you shout at me like that, I don't have to give you a free taxi service from the airport.'

Aysha's father sounded older and more weary than her grandfather had ever been. 'But I always pay my rent at the end of the month.'

'Yes. And you weren't here at the end of August, so it didn't get paid.'

'I'm going to pay him today. I'm an honest man. I've always paid on time.'

Faruk leaned over again and closed the passenger door. 'I know you're an honest man. That's why I feel so bad about it. That's why I came to get you from the airport. It's the least I could do. But I'm not a rich man. I couldn't pay the rent for you. Don't you understand? He's let the house to another family already. He said he'd be ruined if he didn't get his rent.'

Aysha couldn't see the faces of the two men in the front of the car. She could only see her father's shoulders curled forward, as if he was trying to hide himself away in the smallest possible space. In Jamdher, he had looked so strong and so rich and so powerful that she had almost hated him. She had hated him for forcing her to leave Bangladesh and travel across the world to a country whose language was a secret code. Now she felt sorry for him.

'But I bought some new pans,' he said, 'so my wife can cook for me. I've had no one to cook for me all the time I've lived in England.'

Faruk started the engine again. 'I've got your pans and all your bedclothes. Don't worry. You won't be out on the streets. You can stay for a week in this new place I've got. I haven't done it up yet, so the rent will be much less than the house. That'll give you a good start.'

There were two damp mattresses on the floor in Faruk's house and no other furniture at all. But they slept as soon as they got there and only Aysha woke when her father got up five hours later. When she opened her eyes, bright sunshine played with the dust in the room. There were no curtains and outside it had stopped raining.

'I'll have to walk to work,' her father said, 'I've got no English money. Tell your mother I'll bring us something home to eat this evening.' He smiled. 'There's nowhere for us to cook in this house. And she's tired, so tired.'

'When am I going to school?'

Going to school was the only reason Aysha could think of for being in England. It was the only thing Dada would say to her when she pleaded with him not to make her go to England, the only good thing Piara could think of. 'In England you'll get an education. Just think how proud we'll be of you. Just think what you can do for the family if you work hard at school.'

Her father looked at Ama fast asleep and whispered, 'First we must find somewhere to live. Then I'll find you a school. We can't stay here. Faruk needs the room for a cousin of his. But I'll find something. When I get home from work. Now go to sleep.'

The door slammed behind him and the noise stabbed at Aysha's ears, still buzzing from the silence after hours of being in the plane. Still Ama slept. And when Aysha woke again, hungry, at eleven o'clock in the morning, her mother was still asleep.

In her grandfather's house, Aysha's mother was always the first to wake, singing softly as she brought water back from the well for Dadi and made a fire with the wood she'd collected the night before. Aba had promised them they wouldn't have to collect firewood ever again when they lived in England and had talked of the cooker he had in his house where a flame came when you pressed a button. When Dadi didn't believe him, he made her get the radio he had brought as a present and showed her, over and over again, how the sound came out when he pressed a button. 'That's how the cooking works in England too,' he said.

And Dadi had laughed as she watched Ama chopping onions and chillies and said, 'I suppose you press a button to chop the onions too.' She'd said there was no such thing as a flame when you pressed a button and Aysha's grandfather had laughed at her and told her she was a silly old woman. 'They've got machines for everything in England,' he said. 'They won't have to do any work at all once they get to England.'

Aysha felt dirty. She had the same clothes on she had had for the whole journey and Faruk hadn't told them where to wash when they arrived. In Jamdher, she had dressed in shorts like her cousins most of the time, but whenever she did wear a shalwar suit, her mother had always washed her tunic and trousers straight away and hung them up to dry in the hot, fresh air outside in the yard. She had never worn the same clothes for two days without washing.

Old green paint flaked off the walls in the empty house, and the sink which Aysha found was threaded with green and brown tracks of rust and dirt. The water was a rusty colour, too, but at least it was cold and Aysha could wash her face.

Because there were no curtains in the room where they had slept, Aysha stood in the bay window waiting for her mother to wake up. She saw a row of identical houses with broken window frames, some with jagged holes in their windows. The house directly across the narrow street was beautifully painted, with pale blue curtains that rippled horizontally like the waves of the sea, but the house next door to that had grey-green wood which hadn't been painted for twenty years, and curtains held together with dirt. An old woman, an English woman, with a pinched, grey-green face, peered out at Aysha, raising the curtain to cover most of her face as shy country women in Jamdher had hidden behind their saris. As soon as she realized Aysha had seen her, she dropped the curtain and disappeared.

The whole of the street was lined with cars. Packed tightly together, the cars filled both sides of the narrow street so there was barely enough room for any of them to drive down the middle. Aysha watched as a young white woman, an English woman, tried in vain to push a baby's buggy between two cars and then gave up and lifted the baby and the buggy high in the air to cross the street. Aysha smiled. She had never seen a buggy before and it made her think of the rickshaws in Dhaka and Sylhet. The young English woman saw her and smiled back.

Aysha wanted to wake her mother, to show her all the cars and the baby buggy. But Ama had never slept like this before. It would have been wrong to wake her.

When Ama finally did wake up, she was sick and thirsty and didn't want to talk. Aysha was used to her mother being quiet. In Dadi's noisy kitchen, with all her aunts coming and going and the neighbours sitting down for tea and the beggar women travelling through with their news of what was happening in the world outside, Ama had always been the quiet one, serving tea and handing out rice to the beggar women, doing all the jobs that Dadi gave her without complaining. That was her duty, as daughter-in-law, to do whatever her mother-in-law asked. Aysha knew that one day it would be her duty, to be like a servant to her mother-in-law. Dada had promised that he would find her the best mother-in-law in the district.

She wondered what her mother would do now, now that there was no work to do for her grand-mother. She remembered how busy they were in Dadi's kitchen when the rice was harvested, so busy that even Aysha and Komla had to help out. And she remembered how much her aunts and her grand-mother had pitied the wives of men who had no land – because they had so little work to do. In England they would have no land. Ama lay on her side, wide awake now and staring at the dirty wall opposite the window.

29

Aysha wanted to get her mother something to drink, but she had no cup. And the orange-brown water which came out of the tap made her remember her grandmother shouting at them when they drank water from the well without boiling it during the rainy season. There was so much water that the children couldn't even see the point of collecting it from the well. They wanted to cup their hands and take a drink from one of the hundreds of little ponds that sprang up all around the yard. But Dadi had read the pamphlet which Piara brought home from her sewing workshop. The pamphlet had drawings of children lying down, looking very sick and drawings of cooking pots over the fire to show that you should boil the water you wanted to drink.

Aysha was thirsty too, but there was nowhere for her to boil the water. They would have to wait.

By the time her father came home, it was dark outside. Aysha had filled in the hours by counting the times the old woman in the house across the street twitched at the curtain and tried to catch a glimpse of them without them noticing her. Aysha tried to smile at her, but each time the old woman caught sight of Aysha watching, her face melted away behind the dirty curtain like one of the spirits Dadi said were hiding behind the mango trees.

There were no lights in Faruk's house. No lights went on in the old lady's room either. Soon, Aysha could see nothing except for the street lights and the light in the living-room of the house opposite, with curtains like waves of the sea. Sometimes she thought she saw the pinched, grey-white face of the old spirit lady. But she might have been imagining it.

Aysha and her mother were prisoners, prisoners in a strange land. For the first few days, nobody spoke to them and they never went out. It wouldn't have been right for them to go out alone in that strange city. They were short of water and had to sit in the dark when daylight had faded. Once a day Aba opened the front door and brought them some hot food, in silver foil trays, from a shop he passed on his way home from work. It was as if Aba were their jailer.

But he didn't wish them any harm. It was someone else, something else, that was keeping them locked up in the house that smelt of damp and choking dust. Every night, as soon as he came home from work with the silver trays full of hot food, he went out again and locked the door behind him. He was looking for somewhere else for them to live, Ama said, because Faruk had promised the rooms in his house to two other families he knew.

Aysha asked her mother where Aba's furniture was. Back in Jamdher, Dadi always gave the old beggar women much more than rice in exchange for their stories of what was going on in the other villages round about. Aysha had heard her reading aloud to them from her father's letters, explaining to them what a sofa was and what a television was because Dadi pretended to know about all these things, from reading books. And when Aysha read the letters later to her mother, she realized that Dadi had made up a lot of the riches she talked about in her stories, to make Aba's life in London sound even more successful than it was. But she, too, had read in his letters about the sofa and the television. Everyone in the village knew he had a television.

She stood with her mother in the bay window, watching her father disappear down the dark street and whispered, 'Faruk says he has Aba's cooking pots and bedclothes. So where is his television?'

Ama shook her head. 'He told me the truth when I asked him. He told me he never had a house. Only a room. The furniture belonged to his landlord. He thought Dadi would be worried about him if he told us he was only living in one room. He didn't want her to think he was poor. He had to send money to us in Jamdher.'

Aysha moved across to the left of the window and pressed her nose against the glass to see if she could catch a glimpse of her father. They didn't know when he would be back that night from his search for a place for them to live. They had no clock, no other people to ask, no way of knowing.

'We won't be poor,' her mother said. 'Your father's got a good job. Just look at the way he managed to save the fare for us to come here. And the presents he brought for Piara's wedding. But he thought he could stay in that room he's been living in until he found a house for the three of us.'

Aysha longed to go outside. There were no palm trees in the street they looked out on, no green of young paddy fields. There were only a few stiff plane trees losing their tired, smoky yellow leaves and shedding flakes of their bark as a snake sheds its skin. Aysha missed the sounds of the frogs and the crickets at night and in the daytime the sound of all her cousins splashing through Dada's pond, chasing each other for a ball. She even missed the droning sound of their teacher's voice as they sat in rows reciting the Holy Book in Arabic every morning.

The only sound she heard from the front room of Faruk's empty house was the distant buzz of traffic that sometimes became the screeching sound of brakes as the buses rounded a corner she had never seen. Once, the screeching of brakes was followed by an explosive bang and then a deadly silence for a long time before the normal buzz of cars and buses started up again.

For that first week, Aysha and her mother lived as if someone had blotted out the whole of England except for that empty room and the view of the narrow, car-lined street.

One night Aba came home later than ever with the food for them in silver foil trays. He told them he had been to pray at the mosque. It was already Friday and they hadn't even noticed that five days had passed since their arrival in England. He had some good news as well. Someone at work had told him the Housing Office would find them somewhere to live and he had gone there in his lunch break.

'They will put us in a hotel,' he said. It was the first time Aba had stayed long enough in the evening to sit down and eat with them. 'It's called Bed and Breakfast. They give us something to eat in the morning. And then they will let us have a house to rent when they have one empty.'

'And can I go to school?'

Aba was impatient. 'I've got my job to go to. I can't do everything at once. Now I've got to ask

Faruk to drive us over there tomorrow. And we can take the new pans I bought. There's a kitchen there, they said.'

Chapter Four

Aysha couldn't understand a word the man was saying. But neither could her father. He had lived in England for a long, long time. More than fifteen years. She had no idea how long. But still he let the big fat man shout at him and still he didn't shout anything back in English.

It was only after they had lived in London for two weeks that Aysha finally managed to persuade her father to try and find her a school. 'You're such a chatterbox,' he said. 'You're as bad as Dadi. She never stops talking until she gets her way, either. I'll have to take time off work,' he said. 'And we can't afford to lose money. We have to save in case we have to go back to Bangladesh.'

But someone had to go with Aysha. Ama couldn't take her to the school. She couldn't speak English, for a start. And Aba didn't like them to go out on their own. He said it was all right for them to go out in Jamdher, where everybody knew them, but London was full of strangers. He seemed to be frightened all the time that something bad would happen to them if they didn't stay at home with the door locked.

Ama was happier when they moved from Faruk's house to the Bed and Breakfast Hotel but Aba was angry about the place. 'Do they think we are pigs? Worse than pigs?' he said. The Bed and Breakfast

Hotel was five storeys tall, with four rooms and one dirty toilet on each floor. The stairway smelt like a toilet that hasn't been cleaned for weeks. The kitchen, down in the dark, damp basement, had one small light, a bulb on a long string that dangled over a cupboard in the corner. There was one sink and five tiny electric hotplates, but two of them were broken and the other three were never free for Ama to cook. And there was never any breakfast.

At night, the whole house shook with the sounds of babies crying and children fighting and angry men yelling at them to be quiet. Aysha had never heard such anger, had hardly heard babies crying, in Jamdher. When one of her baby cousins cried in her grandfather's house in Jamdher, there had always been someone, an aunt or Dadi, to pick them up and comfort them. But in the Bed and Breakfast Hotel the same tiny cries went on for hours and hours until loud men's voices shouted abuse from other rooms and the crying was stopped for a time or got louder and more frightened.

One day, five police cars drew up in front of the house and, from the landing window, Aysha saw four more policemen out at the back, climbing over the rubbish against the dirty yellow brick wall. There were eight policemen out at the front, two of them big, fat men who talked into phones all the time. The policemen in uniform took away a thin, pale white woman with a short, tight skirt that clung to her grey and purple bruised legs. Three hours later another police car came and a policewoman got out. And they took away the two red-haired children who had been sitting outside on the crumbling steps to the house ever since their mother had gone.

It was a violent house, a house full of anger and noise and dirt and hunger. But Aysha's mother was happier there.

There was another Bangladeshi woman in the Bed and Breakfast Hotel, living with her four children in the room next to theirs, so that Aysha and her mother could move back and forth between the two rooms. Zahida was better than they were at making sure she got a turn to cook in the kitchen because she could speak English and bossed the other women about. So she often cooked for them and they ate together upstairs in her room.

Aysha's mother felt sorry for Zahida because her husband had died a year after she arrived in England. 'She has no man to look after her,' Ama said. 'All her brothers are in Bangladesh and her son is too young to support her. What will happen to her now?'

But Aysha didn't see why they should feel sorry for Zahida. When Aysha and her mother had first gone down to the kitchen, two women in there had hurled angry words at them, forcing them back to their room. They were scared and helpless, not knowing what they had done wrong. But Zahida could speak English. She could stand up for herself. She could tell people what she needed and argue with the landlord of the hotel if he shouted at any of her children. She went to the Housing Office every week and told them she needed a proper place to live. And she went to a college to learn dressmaking, every day when her children were at school.

'There's no shame in it, sister,' she said to Aysha's

mother, who had been brought up to believe that only a man should go out into the world and deal with the world outside the house. 'It would be much more shameful if I let my children stay in a house like this because I don't have a man to speak for me.'

Zahida could speak English better than Aysha's father. But that was something Aysha only found out when he finally took a day off work to go and ask about a school for her. The commissionaire at the Town Hall had a smart, dark uniform on, like a soldier or a policeman.

'Have you got an appointment?'

'I want a school for my daughter.'

'Have you got an appointment?'

'Is this where I get a school? They told me I have to come here to get a school.'

'Look, who do you want to see, mate? You can't just walk in here. You've got to have an appointment.' The commissionaire started to shout, as if Aysha's father were deaf. He was still holding his pen and had his newspaper open at the crossword puzzle. In between asking questions, he looked down at his paper and started to read again. Then he put his pen behind his ear.

'Look, make up your mind, mate. Do you want to see someone here, or do you want to see someone from the Education Offices? If you want to see someone here, you should have an appointment. Have you got a letter or something?'

Aysha's father shook his head. 'Just a school for my daughter. Is this the right place?'

The commissionaire came out from behind the gate which led to his desk. He was wearing grubby, grey

38

trainers. Twice as tall as Aysha's father, he took hold of him by both shoulders and turned him round to face the glass doors. Then he spoke very loudly, taking a deep breath between each word.

'Look, mate,' he said, 'if it's the Education Offices you want, you go out of these doors. Then you turn right.' As he said, 'right', he lifted up Aba's right arm as if he were a puppet and pointed it to the right. 'Then you bear left, go under the subway and take the exit marked Bus Station. Then you go round the roundabout, through the underpass and it's straight ahead. You can't miss it. A big ugly old building with a dome on top. Dome. Got it?' The phone rang and he dropped Aba's arm and went back through the little gate to his desk.

'Got it? Dome. Ed-u-cation Office,' he said. Then he picked up the phone.

It was already eleven o'clock and Aba was impatient. 'I can't afford to lose the afternoon's pay as well as this morning,' he said. 'I might even lose my job if I'm not careful.'

They had to ask a lot more people before they found the Education Offices. There was a man in the market who spoke their dialect. 'Why did you come this way?' he said to them. 'You've gone completely out of your way if you want the Education Offices.' By the time they got to the building with the dome on top it was nearly twelve.

The woman at the desk inside the door said she was sorry she couldn't speak Bengali, but she could speak Urdu with Aba if he wanted. He said he preferred to speak English. Slowly, repeating every word

39

twice, she explained that there wouldn't be anyone in the office to see parents of new pupils until two.

Aysha's father refused to stay at the office any longer.

'But Aysha needs to go to school,' Ama said when they got back to their room in the dirty hotel. Aysha had never seen her mother arguing with a man before.

'I can't miss work,' her father said. 'Do you want me to lose my job?'

Aysha was helpless. Back home in Jamdher, she had always managed to do what she really wanted to. And she really wanted to go to school. Dada, her uncles, everyone said she could talk the birds out of the trees. But all her language was useless to her now. The people in the offices, the people in the hotel, everyone treated her as if she were deaf and dumb. Everything they had to say, to her or about her, they said through her father. And they treated him as if he were stupid.

All her life, Aysha had known that she could depend on the head of the household, on Dada, to make sure she had everything she needed. They had had enough to eat from his land and a good house to live in. Everyone for miles around had come to her grandfather for help and advice. She had had plenty of friends and Dadi had taught them to read whenever the roads were too flooded to go to school. But Dada was thousands of miles away. Now her father was head of the household.

Aysha wanted to help her family. She wanted to help her mother get away from that dirty, loud house where they were never alone and only ever among friends when Zahida was there. She wanted to do things for herself so her father didn't get sick with worry because he had to take time off work and take her to look for a school. It was her duty to help her family. But as long as she couldn't speak English there was nothing she could do.

Chapter Five

Aysha had never seen such beautiful shops, real shops with plate-glass window panes and a rainbow of saris and fabrics for shalwar suits. The vegetable shops spilled okhra and garlic and onions out on to the pavements, where old women in white saris prodded at the ginger and chillies and water melons piled high on green baskets. Tiny girls in fluffy pink dresses were dragged along, clutching their mothers' hands and babies sat in buggies slurping away at ice pops and being ignored. Ghandi's Carpet Emporium sold bracelets by the yard and plastic flowers and posters of Hindi films and dishcloths and doormats and comics, but there wasn't a carpet in sight. There were chemist's shops with racks and racks of videos with Urdu titles that Aysha could just about read and jewellers' with golden collars and earrings and wedding jewels brilliant on red velvet cushions. The whole of the High Street smelt of spices and excitement, and the air danced to the tune of twenty or more different languages.

Ama stood with her face pressed to the window of a jeweller's shop. 'How many rich people are there in London?' she asked. 'Who has the money to buy all this?' And Aba led them proudly past Sabina's Designer Shalwar Suits to the jeweller's next door. 'This is where I bought Piara's bracelet,' he said. Ama gasped and Aysha stared at the rows of gold bracelets resting on red velvet. 'I couldn't let my only sister look poor when she got married,' he said.

Aba took them out shopping to the High Street once a week, on Saturday afternoons when the factory where he worked was closed. When Ama needed fresh food during the week, Aysha's father went out on his own after work to the shops on every street corner that were open until midnight. He always grumbled because it was dark and cold and late at night, but he didn't want them going to the shops on their own. He said that people back home would think they were poor if his wife and daughter had to trail the streets of London without a man. 'I may have to work hard,' he said, 'but at least I can afford to look after you properly.'

Then one day Aysha's mother sent her out to the shops on her own. They knew that Aba wouldn't like it, so they didn't tell him. But Zahida went out to the shops all the time. She had no one else to go shopping for her. Zahida said that was why she could speak good English – because she had no one else to speak English for her.

At first, Aysha only went to the vegetable shop on the corner of their street when her mother needed garlic or onions. The woman there spoke Punjabi to her children, but she spoke English to Aysha, slowly, repeating things and holding up the vegetables after Aysha pointed to them. Soon, Aysha was picking up things she didn't need to buy and showing them to Mrs Mehtab, just so she could learn their names in English.

Mrs Mehtab didn't sell good rice so that after a

43

while, if Aysha had to buy rice, her mother would tell her to go to a special shop in the High Street where the rice was better – though it was never as good as the rice they husked themselves from Dada's fields. When Aysha's mother started to talk about Dada's rice, she didn't stop till she had brought Jamdher back with her talk – the taste of rice cooked well, the smell of the fresh grain when they brought the rice into the yard, all the hard work they had to do during the rice harvest. She talked of the sound of Dadi's kitchen, the drumming sound as all the women in the village sat working the dheki, the board they used to husk the rice before they cooked it. Aysha and Komla had made their own toy dhekis when they were small, and pretended to work like their mothers.

Aba was annoyed when they talked about Jamdher. If he heard them talking about the rice he would say, 'You should be grateful that you don't have to spend hours husking rice any more. This is progress. All you have to do here is buy it from the shops. Your problem is, you have too little work to do. If you had to work as I do, you wouldn't keep moaning about the things you miss in Jamdher.'

Aysha's mother missed her work. And Aysha missed running in the fields with her cousins. She was only really happy when she could get out of the loud, dirty, five-storey Bed and Breakfast Hotel, outside and down to the streets and the shops. She longed to go to school.

On his second visit to the Education Offices, Aba was told he would have to come back and see about a school when they had a proper place to live. 'There's not much point in us finding her a place in one of our schools if you're going to be moved to another part of London in a few weeks,' the woman in the office smiled.

The next day they were moved to another part of London. But it wasn't because the Housing Office had found them a house. It was because the people at the office had found out that Aba's room where he had lived for ten years was in a different London borough. So they said that Aba would have to go to a different Housing Office.

Zahida had finally got a flat, so she was leaving the Bed and Breakfast Hotel too. Aysha and her mother helped her into the taxi with her two suitcases and her children. Then they waved goodbye and thanked her for all she had done for them and promised they would go to visit her in her new flat. But they didn't realize how big London was, and they never saw her again.

The Eastern Promise Motel was built by the side of one of the busiest roads in London. Behind it, a factory clattered and boomed all day and all night, with hooters like air-raid sirens six times a day telling the shift workers when to start and stop their work. In front of the Motel, at the other side of a buckled, crumpled fence, buses and lorries and queues of cars whistled or groaned or screeched past, their droning rhythm occasionally knocked out of tune by the violent chainsaw sound of a motor bike. At night, at midnight, at three o'clock in the morning, it felt as if the dual carriageway passed straight through the room where Aysha slept with her parents. Car doors slammed and drunken men shouted greetings to one another as they arrived to spend the night in one of the few motel rooms not occupied by homeless families.

The walls, the beds, even the sheets were much thinner than in the Bed and Breakfast Hotel. On the first night, when Aysha couldn't sleep for the noise outside, she tossed and turned and heard ripping sounds, as the tiny holes her mother had noticed in the sheets turned her bed into a tattered heap.

'I hope we don't have to pay for that,' Aba said. 'I've already missed two days off work. I just haven't got any money to spare.'

They weren't allowed to stay in the motel all day. From ten o'clock in the morning until five o'clock at night they had to leave their rooms empty. But there was nowhere to go. Aba went to the Housing Office again, pleading with them to give him a place where his wife and daughter could stay during the day. They asked him why Ama didn't go to English classes at the Tech. Then they said Aysha couldn't go to the English classes with her mother because she was too young.

'She'll have to go to school,' they said. 'You're breaking the law,' they said, 'if you don't send her to school.' Aba told them how keen she was to go to school and how he'd tried to get her a school, but the woman at the Housing Office, with one eye on the clock and the other on the long queue of people behind Aysha's father said, 'You'll have to talk to the Education Offices about that. That's not down to us. It's down to the Education Offices.'

'But I can't send my wife and daughter out all day while I am at work.'

'That's all we can do. The motel is all we've got for temporary accommodation at the moment. You could try making your own arrangements.'

November in London was colder and greyer than anything Aysha had ever known, but people still said it was mild weather for the time of year. There was no pavement near the motel, only a filthy subway leading under the road, which emerged at the other side to a street of boarded-up houses, with broken glass framing the rain-soaked grey wooden boards at the windows. Aba had to leave for work at seven every morning and didn't get back till after six, so he never saw them wandering around looking for somewhere to keep warm.

One day they passed a building with white steps leading up to a large double door, where a sign in lots of different languages, even in Bengali, said, 'Welcome'. Aysha laughed and said that meant they could go inside, but her mother told her not to be stupid. The red-brick building with a glass dome on top and its entrance hall with a pattern of flowers in red and white tiles was more beautiful than any of the grey tower blocks and run-down terraced houses round about. Ama thought it was only a place for rich people.

So they stood outside and stared at it and then walked on to a park where there were donkeys and ducks and geese penned in behind a very high fence. They walked past the high fences of schools as well, where children played and scuffled with each other on the tough black tarmac of the playground. Like prisoners allowed out in an exercise yard, Aysha and her mother watched what was happening in the real world through high wire fences.

A woman with red hair came to the motel and talked to them once a week. She was there to see lots of the people who lived in the motel, all hoping she would bring them news of a place to live or a place to work. As soon as she arrived, she was surrounded by women and men who had no jobs to go to and no place to go during the day, shouting at her and complaining about the noise from the rooms next door to theirs. Miss Atkins had very white skin and hair the deep orange colour of an over-ripe mango. Every time she came, she smiled her lovely freckled smile at Aysha and her mother and said, 'Are you all right? I'm really sorry I can't speak Bengali but if there's anything I can do . . .' And Aysha's mother smiled back at her – she was such a nice English lady – and said, 'All right.'

As long as the weather stayed mild, being out of doors was better than being forced to stay inside all day, in Faruk's empty house or in the noisy Bed and Breakfast Hotel. Every day they went to the park and looked in at the door of the building with the grand flight of steps and the glass dome on top. They found another High Street, like the one near the Bed and Breakfast Hotel, where Ama could examine all the things in all the shops, even though they never had any money to buy.

Then one day they woke up to find it snowing. Aysha had a thin, pink anorak that Aba had come home with one night from his factory. Ama had a proper coat because Zahida had given her one in October when they had no idea how cold it could be

48

in England. But both of them only had loose sandals on their feet. And at ten o'clock they had to leave the motel. The other people staying there crowded round the reception desk shouting at the woman who answered the telephones and Aysha heard the woman repeat the same words she used every day, every time people asked to stay in the motel. 'It's not down to me. I don't make the rules. If it was down to me, I'd let you stay in all day myself. But they've got this arrangement with the Housing Department. I think it's diabolical, myself. But it's not down to me.'

Aysha and her mother didn't stop to argue. They knew the rules. The snow by the dual carriageway was already a filthy grey-black sludge when they had to wade through it to get to the subway. Aysha dug her hands into her pockets. The snow would have been all right if only there hadn't been a fierce wind blowing the cold right through her. 'We'll have to go to the shopping centre,' her mother said, 'where it's covered over, out of the wind.' But it usually took them more than an hour to walk to the covered shopping centre and they hadn't found the quick way there.

Aysha had been shivering since they stepped out of the motel and into the wind but by the time they reached the building near the park, with the glass dome on top, her whole body was shaking. She couldn't talk. She just wanted to sit down on the cold steps and wait till the violent shaking stopped. Her mother fought to stop her sitting down.

'You can't stay here. It's still too cold. We've got to go to the shopping centre.'

Aysha smiled. She wanted to go to sleep. She knew

that if she didn't sit down, she would fall down. She smiled at her mother and sat down on the bottom step and then couldn't hear her mother's voice any more. A drumming sound, like the drumming of the dhekis husking rice beat in her ears and she saw her mother's face coming and going as if she were dancing. Then her mother was screaming.

A face came towards her, the large, round, red face of a man with a thin ring of grey hair round his polished pink head. Blue eyes. White teeth. 'Come along. We can't leave her out here.'

Aysha felt herself being lifted and carried and placed on a soft, soft bed and still she was shaking. Her arms and legs were shaking as if they didn't belong to her. She thought she should stop shivering now she was lying on the deep, soft bed. But her arms and legs had no connection with what she thought.

A woman's voice, calm, not her mother's, came and went, came and went, and a warm, thick, soft quilt wrapped itself round her. Her mother was crying and still Aysha's arms and legs and her shoulders were roughly shaking her in and out of sleep. The calm voice in English came closer and someone rubbed at Aysha's hands, each of them separately until they were warm and then her feet, one by one and then the whole thing over again because as soon as the warm hands stopped massaging Aysha's hands and arms, her shoulders began their violent shivering over again.

She heard the word, 'Doctor', and her mother saying, 'Thank you, thank you', and then crying. And the words in Bengali began to make sense again. 'We shouldn't have come to England. England will kill my

50

daughter.' And then Ama cried, over and over again, 'We can't let Dada see us now. We musn't let Dada know how poor we are. It would break his heart.' And she cried again and the calm voice in English stroked and warmed Aysha back to consciousness and calmed her mother down.

They made her sit up and drink, when she had stopped shivering, though Aysha wanted more than anything else to drift away to sleep and dream of playing with her cousins, running in and out of the sunny courtyard where clothes dried five minutes after you had put them out. She wanted to be left alone to dream of splashing about in the warm rain or sitting in Dada's house with the kerosene light on, listening to the crickets sing and Dada tell one of his stories of the time he fought in the British Army. But they wouldn't let her sleep. They made her drink a kind of milk that was warm and far too sweet and the colour of a coconut shell. And she looked round the room.

It was a dark corridor full of books on shelves that reached to the ceiling, with a patch of light from a window at the end. A woman with a pale pink face and pale grey hair was holding the cup of cocoa for Aysha to drink and smiled at her with eyes that bulged behind very thick glasses. 'That's more like it,' she said, 'I think she's going to be all right now.' She held her watch very close to Aysha's face. 'But it's taken more than an hour to warm you up, young lady. That'll teach you to go out without the proper clothing.' Under the library store-room window, all three bars of an electric fire radiated heat towards the old settee where Aysha was lying.

'And the vicar brought you his quilt,' the woman continued, 'and everyone out there keeps asking about you. None of them'll leave till they know you're all right again.'

She kept on talking, hardly pausing for breath, as if Aysha and her mother were understanding every word she said. And through all that hail of strange new words Aysha understood the warmth and understood that someone cared about them.

After that, they went to the library every day except Sunday. On Sunday, when Aba had no work to go to, they kept warm in a great big do-it-yourself centre that was open till late. The shop assistants followed them and watched them because they never bought anything. Someone was always there, watching them as they walked along the rows of tools and paintbrushes, paints and screwdrivers – hundreds of tools they had never seen, hundreds of wallpapers and furniture kits for other people's houses.

When the library began to close early on Saturday, they didn't complain. Instead, they took shelter in the covered market and walked around the vegetable stalls until they knew it was time to go back to the motel. But nowhere was as warm and welcoming as the library.

There were books in Bengali there, so Aysha could read aloud quietly to her mother. And there were books full of beautiful photos, so that it didn't matter that they were in languages Aysha couldn't yet read.

It wasn't only books they went for. They were starting to get to know people there. Every day they saw the same old men, who sat for hours in the reading room with a newspaper open in front of them. One old man, who sat with a dictionary open beside his newspaper, sniffed all day as if he always had a cold and only stopped sniffing when he fell asleep. Aysha noticed two more old men who came to talk to each other and not to read and she tried to listen to what they said. The very small thin man talked so fast that Aysha couldn't catch a word of what he said, but the other man sat and nodded his head and simply said, 'Oh yeah?' The only other thing she ever heard him say was, 'Cold out, isn't it?' whenever he arrived to take his seat. And the tall man said, 'Warm in here, though.'

The librarian told them they couldn't join the library until they had a proper place to live. But that was a luxury they could only dream of, being able to take books home. For the moment, it was enough that they had found a place where they could be warm and dry during the day, a place where Aysha knew her mother could be safe when she finally started school.

Chapter Six

Aysha knew what school was like. She had been to the school in Jamdher for four years. She had seen the High School too, because Dada had wanted to send her there before he knew they would have to move to England. The school in Jamdher was a place where the walls were clean and whitewashed inside, where the children sat in rows on benches, the boys on one side and the girls on the other, holding slates on their knees to write on. School was a place which was sometimes almost silent while the older children read in whispers to the younger ones they were helping to read. Sometimes school was loud with the one voice of fifty children reciting the same lesson after the teacher. But the best thing about school for Aysha was the friends she played with at school and then the games she played all the way home with her cousins, all of the boys and Komla.

The English school her father had chosen was a school which was only for girls. Faruk had told him that the boys were very bad in England and that she shouldn't go to a school with boys. Faruk had offered to go with them the first day she was due at school, so he could help her father to understand what the teachers told them. He read the letter they received and told them it meant they had to go to the Education Offices first at nine o'clock in the morning.

'Haven't I been there enough?' Aba said. But they got there very early and waited outside for Faruk to arrive.

When Faruk arrived at half past nine, he said he had had to go shopping first for his wife. Then he pushed his way through the swing doors without waiting for them and went up to the desk, waving the letter they'd got about Aysha's school. Aysha and her father saw the woman pointing to the letter and speaking very slowly as she explained to Faruk that the letter came from the Education Office but that they weren't supposed to go there. They were supposed to go to the school.

'And anyway, you're late,' she said. Even Faruk, clever Faruk, who did business with the English people, couldn't read their letters.

There were two offices at Florence Nightingale School and the first one they went to was the wrong one. Girls in grey uniforms stared at them as a teacher rushed with them across the road to the office on the other side. 'That was the Upper School,' she said, talking to them as if they were small children. 'It's the Lower School you want. Lower School. But are you sure it's this school you want to send her to? She's very small.'

'She's nearly thirteen,' Faruk said.

The secretary in the office was bored. She picked up the phone as soon as they arrived and left them standing at a little window while she spoke to someone else about them.

'Got another girl here to see Miss Sykes. They're always late,' she said, 'they've just got no idea of the time. Shall I send them up?'

Then she put down the phone and told them they were too late. She said the teacher who'd made an appointment to see them was too busy and they'd have to come back the following day. And even then, Aysha was told she couldn't start till the following week.

Faruk's wife, Anwara, sewed her a silver-grey shalwar kameez because they were allowed to wear anything to school as long as it was grey. And on Monday morning she walked with her mother past the library to the same school office she had been to with her father.

Going to school was the reason they had made her come to England, her grandmother and grandfather and Piara. They had told her that in England she could go to a good school and have much better chances. Everyone said that if she worked hard enough she might even get to work for the government in Dhaka, where she could live with her uncle. Aysha knew that they wouldn't have made her go away with a father she hardly knew if it wasn't good for the family, if they hadn't believed in her and how well she would do once she got the chance to go to a good school.

The school in Jamdher had always been quiet and calm at the reading time, first thing in the morning. But Aysha's new London school buzzed, screeched, shouted, squawked, yelled, and tore at the air. After she had watched her mother walk away, past the park and back towards the library, she put her hands over her ears and stood with her eyes closed outside the school office, not knowing what to do next. Girls, all of them much bigger than her, pushed past her waving shiny red books. They opened the office door, threw the red registers inside and slammed the door behind them, rushing off down the corridor and shouting as if their friends were right up at the top of a tall tree instead of walking next to them.

A bell like a fire engine hammered away on top of the sounds of girls shouting and screeching, and teachers in jeans rushed past clutching their registers and dropping their books. Then all of a sudden there was silence.

Aysha pushed open the door of the office.

'Please.'

The secretary pushed a cream doughnut back inside a paper bag. She went on reading the newspaper she held in one hand and picked up a green form with her other hand. 'You're supposed to knock. And anyway, girls who need a late slip have to come to the window.'

'Please. My name is Aysha.'

'Aysha what?'

'Aysha Begum.'

'Not another one! I don't know how I'm supposed to tell who's who, with all you Begums.' She laughed as if she had made a joke, and Aysha smiled at her. But she didn't understand.

A teacher came into the room behind Aysha and tapped her on the shoulder. 'I think this is Aysha,' she said, 'I've come to collect her. Have you got her form?'

The secretary let out a great sigh, as if she had just put down a heavy load of shopping. 'Well, I'm glad you've come. I never know what to do with them. Another one of them Bengalis, is it? How am I supposed to find the forms when they've all got the same names? What form'll she be in?'

'Second Year.'

'Bit small . . .' The secretary continued to stick paper clips between her cyclamen-coloured lips as she sorted through the forms she had been given the day before. 'Is this it?' she said, 'Aysha Begum?'

'Oh God!' The teacher pointed to the words in green felt-tip that someone had written in large, block capitals across the front of the form.

It said, AYSHA BEGUM – NO LANGUAGE.

'That's right, isn't it?' The secretary still had a moustache of sugar from the doughnut she'd been eating. 'She can't speak no English. Another one of them with no language. I don't know how you manage to teach them anything. It's too hard on all the teachers, having all these that don't speak no English. Rather you than me.'

The teacher opened the door of a room so narrow and high it made Aysha feel dizzy to look up at the ceiling. They took two steps inside.

'This is Aysha Begum,' she said, 'I hope you'll all be nice to her. Mr McAllan?'

From somewhere at the back of the classroom, as if he had been folded up tightly in a box and hidden away, a thin, pale man suddenly shot to the front. He wasn't very old, but strands of grey stippled hair whisked around his head like satellites as he walked. Wisps of sandy-coloured hair tried hard to look like a beard on his thin, pointed chin. He wore grey jeans and the sleeves of his lumber-jack shirt were rolled up to the elbows. Through the gap at the front of his shirt where a button was missing, his chest showed white, covered with sandy hair.

The minute he went out of the room with Miss Sykes, twenty-seven pairs of brown eyes and one pair of blue eyes descended on Aysha, like a crowd of butterflies hovering over a flower. Then, just as quickly, the eyes lost interest in her and twenty-eight voices zoomed round the room, fighting for air space in fifteen different languages.

Mr McAllan shot back in, flapping Aysha's form with the green, felt-tipped words on the front, large enough for everyone to read, 'AYSHA BEGUM – NO LANGUAGE'.

'Eh . . . Ger-uls.' He clapped his hands.

From her visits to the shops, from their stay at the motel and from the days she had spent keeping warm in the library with Ama, Aysha could already understand a lot of English. But Mr McAllan, the English teacher, spoke a different language altogether.

'Ger-uls!'

No matter how often he called to them, the girls carried on talking. Aysha was shocked. She remembered how she and Komla had been beaten at the Q'ran school because the Imam caught them whispering. That wasn't right either, the beating. Dada had kept them at home for a month and let them chant their lessons in Arabic to Dadi until the school got a new teacher who wouldn't beat the pupils. But Aysha had never come across a school where the pupils completely ignored their teacher.

'Eh . . . Ger-uls. Can we have a bit of silence, please. Just for a minute.' Mr McAllan shot backwards and forwards at the front of the narrow classroom like a cotamundi in a cage that's too small, his satellite curls swinging like tails. Suddenly he sprang on them.

'Ger-uls! If I don't have silence for a few seconds . . .' Twenty-eight voices were all of a sudden switched off while the sound of the loose change Mr McAllan clinked in the pockets of his loose jeans came through loud and clear.

'Just a few seconds' silence, if you please.' He grinned and then shot to the back of the classroom, where he patted a girl on the shoulder. She wasn't an English girl. None of the girls were English, as far as Aysha could tell, except for a girl on the front row who was big and white, so big that she looked as if she didn't quite know what to do with the length of her arms and legs and so white that she looked as if she spent all her days sitting in a darkened room.

'Shahanara.' Mr McAllan sat on the edge of the desk at the back and grinned again, showing chain-smoker's teeth. 'You speak Bengali, don't you? Stand up when I'm talking to you.'

Shahanara had the prettiest face Aysha had ever seen and long black hair that cascaded from two sparkling hair combs. She was wearing a white lace blouse, with a grey pleated skirt that just touched her knees and long, white, lacy socks.

'I don't speak her sort of Bengali,' Shahanara said, pouting in Aysha's direction and refusing to look at her.

'Listen, Shahanara, I'll have none of your lip. Sit down.' Mr McAllan was up at the front of the room again before Shahanara had taken her seat, carefully smoothing the pleats at the back of her skirt before she sat down.

'Now, look, ger-uls. Aysha here can't speak a word of English. She'll need someone to look after her to make sure she doesn't get lost and I'm asking you, Shahanara, to look after her. That's not too much to ask. Right?'

'Why me, sir? It's not fair!'

'Because you speak Bengali and no one else does.'

'How do you know I speak Bengali?'

'Ach! Come on, Shahanara! Stop messing about.'

'Well, Fatima speaks it as well.'

Fatima's screech made the panes of glass in the long, narrow windows rattle like chattering teeth.

'I never! You liar, Shahanara! You're just trying to get me in trouble.'

Aysha stood still by the door, watching and waiting for the teacher to tell her where to sit.

Shahanara smiled her prettiest smile. 'At least your mum and dad come from the same place as her, Fatima Begum. My mum and dad don't come from Bangladesh, sir,' she said, her smile as sweet as a cupful of sugar rammed down your throat. 'They come from Calcutta. So I don't really speak her language, sir. It's a different dialect, you see.'

Mr McAllan was tired of arguing. He wanted to get back to the back of the classroom where he had been sitting when Aysha arrived, to get back to the book he had been reading while some of the girls got on with the work he had set them and others messed around.

'Look, Shahanara, I don't care what bloomin' dialect you speak to her. All I know is that you can speak to her better than I can and I'm asking you to look after her. Is that too much to ask? As long as Amina's absent, Aysha can sit next to you. Now, Aysha, you go and sit at the back there. Shahanara will look after you.'

Shahanara mumbled that she had work to do and put her head down and began to write, in a furious scrawl that cut through the last remaining pages of her tattered jotter. When Aysha sat down in the seat next to her, she tossed her curls to the other side and turned to face the girl in the seat across the aisle. All the girls were writing or talking but nobody talked to Aysha or told her what to do.

When the hammering bell rang out for break, Shahanara stalked out of the classroom and ran away down the corridor, laughing with her friends. Aysha got lost and didn't know where she was supposed to go until she saw the huge white girl standing up above a sea of faces in the corridor. She followed her, and kept on following Angela when they had to go to the science room and the maths block across the road. But at lunchtime Angela, too, disappeared and Aysha wandered around trying to look as if she knew where she was going.

She wished she could walk away from the school, away from the crowds of shouting girls enjoying themselves, playing football on the green and hide and seek near the dustbins, sharing bags of crisps and stories of what the teachers had done that morning. Aysha had never felt so lonely as she did there in the middle of hundreds of girls, when all of them had their friends and none of them wanted to talk to her. She wished she could walk out of the school and go and find her mother in the library. But dinner ladies in blue nylon overalls stood guard over all the gates, arguing with girls who wanted to go out, and linking arms with girls who just wanted to stop for a chat with them. Aysha wished that she could stand and talk to the friendly-looking woman by the gate near the zebra-crossing, a big woman with red hair and half a dozen first years hanging on her arms. But it was no good trying to talk.

Aysha had nothing to say. All the words she had ever known, all the jokes she had ever told, had been taken away from her. In Jamdher everyone had talked of how clever she was and how she was bound to bring honour to her family by doing well at school. In London, they treated her with pity, as if she could neither hear nor speak. Back in their village, Dada had said that no one could make him laugh like she could. In her London school, Aysha could hear them laughing and none of the laughter made sense.

'Are you all right?' Angela walked through the gate.

'Yes. All right,' Aysha smiled. She knew what all right meant. Over and over again, she had heard the woman in the library telling people, 'Aysha's all right now. Look. She's sitting over there.' Over and over again, the old men who came to the library every day had asked, 'Are you all right now, young lady? You didn't look very well that day the vicar brought you in from the snow.' And Aysha and her mother smiled and said, 'Yes. All right.'

'Hey! You can speak English!' Angela had a smile like a small child who's just been given a large lollipop. She spoke more slowly, 'What's your name?'

'Aysha.'

'Are you on home dinners too?'

Aysha didn't understand her, so Angela said the word dinner again and, 'Did you go home for dinner?' Then she pretended to eat. Aysha shook her head and smiled. No one had shown her the way to the dining hall – but she had got used to going without anything to eat in the middle of the day.

'Oh, you're on school dinners,' Angela said. She took Aysha with her towards the dining hall and showed her inside the door where the dinner ladies were wiping the tables and singing as they did the washing up behind the long stainless steel counter. 'This is where you had your dinner, isn't it?' Angela said.

Aysha smiled and said, 'Yes. All right.'

'Hey! Your English is all right! You understand everything I say,' said Angela, and tucked her arm through Aysha's. 'Do you want to be my friend?'

Aysha smiled. 'Yes. All right.'

Chapter Seven

Angela was big and friendly and lovely. But she couldn't add up. When Aysha was put in the bottom group for maths, Angela was thrilled. 'You don't have to worry about maths now,' she said, 'I'll help you. I'm class monitor.'

Angela was always first to arrive at any of their lessons. While the others girls dawdled, eating crisps on their way upstairs and dropping their schoolbags from the sixth floor right down on to the girls who had just started to climb the stairs, Angela pounded and panted her way up to the maths department. Aysha followed close behind, knowing that if she lost Angela she would be pushed in every direction by nine hundred giggling, yelling, fighting girls and never find her way to the lesson.

Angela even had the key to the maths teacher's cupboard. By the time the others drifted in, two by two and some in threes and then the stragglers on their own, she had got out all the ragged text books and sorted them into a neat pile with all their spines facing the same way. Every time she got the books out she grumbled to Aysha about the other class that used their set of books and always put them back in a mess.

'Look at this mess!' she said. 'They leave the cupboard in a right mess!' But she liked being class monitor.

The other girls sat sleeping off the video of the night before, jaws clamped by elbows firmly planted on the desks, with just enough movement between their hands and their cheeks to chew gum. Angela moved quickly, laying out neat plies of all the different kinds of paper they would need for the maths lesson on the edge of the teacher's desk. And as she did so, she said the names out loud to Aysha, 'Graph paper. That's what we use when we do them graphs. Lined paper. That's for writing. Squared paper. That's for sums. I usually have this one with big squares, 'cos of me writing, 'cos I write big. Miss'll probably let you have that as well.'

At the school in Jamdher, they did their maths on slates. Aysha had never seen so much paper in her life before – beautiful, clean, white paper, with a clean grid of green lines, plain white paper with not a mark on it, just longing to be filled with a beautiful design, writing paper with blue lines, just waiting to be written on.

And then there were the pencils, a whole box of shining red-painted lead pencils. Angela fussed as she sharpened the few that had been used by the class before them. 'You'd think they'd sharpen them before they put them back.' And there were coloured felt-tip pens, thick ones and thin ones thrown together in coloured plastic trays. Angela got out a wooden rack of scissors and a red plastic rack with sticks of glue all standing up straight. 'Shush, you lot,' she said, and rearranged the scissors so they were all facing in the right direction. 'Miss is coming.'

Aysha didn't know where to sit, so she stood next to Angela, helping her to straighten the pencils and sort out the thick felt-tips from the thin. She couldn't believe her luck that a girl who was so important should want to be her friend. Then the door slammed, chairs scraped back, girls stood up and the chewing gummed gums froze as Miss Arkwright marched to the front of the classroom.

Silence. Scared stiff silence.

Behind the silence, distant slamming doors, saucepans slamming in the Home Ec. room, hands clapping in the drama room. Breathing. Then Michelle coughed. Rehana and Amima tried to hide their sniggers in crumpled, days-old paper hankies and Miss Arkwright's ruler hit the desk like a lion-tamer's whip.

'This is not good enough, ladies.'

Her voice was a bark, a dry, rough bark, like a big cat coughing up lumps of fur.

'Now, I want you to go outside again and come back in, in a manner that shows you are ready to start work.'

Nobody looked her in the eye. Eyes drawn down to the floor, the twenty-five girls filed out and stood in a line outside the classroom. Then they looked at the wall, at the door, at the armour-plated grey of her short, sharp hair, until she nodded and they filed back in again, silently, and sat down at their desks. Twenty minutes of the maths lesson had already been taken care of. Maths was Aysha's favourite subject.

'Right. You all know what you're doing. I don't want any more nonsense.'

Miss Arkwright took her seat behind the table at

the front of the classroom and noticed Aysha for the first time.

'Who are you?'

'She can't speak no English, miss.' Michelle had started to cut out paper pentagons and reached over to the teacher's desk to get a stick of glue. 'She don't understand nothing.'

'Oh yes, she does!' Angela said.

'Let's see if she can speak for herself, shall we?' Miss Arkwright spoke suddenly slowly and gently to Aysha, as if she were a small child. 'What's your name?'

Aysha had answered that question a hundred times already since their arrival in England. And every time she told a teacher in the school her name, they said, 'Very Good!' or 'Well Done!' as if it was somehow an amazing achievement to know your own name. Miss Arkwright simply said, 'Any relation to Luthfa Begum?' She nodded across to a fat girl with short hair and dangly earrings who sat at the back of the room.

Luthfa made a face as if she was about to throw up. 'No way!' she said and smiled as her friends all laughed with her.

'Right, I'll have those earrings, Luthfa.' Miss Arkwright held out her hand. 'You know you're not supposed to wear them in school.'

Aysha was watching Angela. All the girls were cutting carefully round the different geometric shapes they had coloured and showing how they tessellated by gluing them on larger sheets of paper. But Angela had a different, bigger pair of scissors. She held the scissors with her left hand and produced pentagons which looked more like circles drawn by a drunken compass. When she reached over to get the glue on the teacher's desk in front of her she sent the racks of glue and scissors sprawling all over the floor.

Miss Arkwright flashed her sharp eyes around the room, as if, for a split second, she expected the other girls to roar with laughter. But nobody laughed at Angela. And Miss Arkwright didn't shout. Instead she said to Aysha, very slowly, 'You'll help Angela to pick them up, won't you, Aysha?'

Aysha smiled and said, 'Yes, Miss. All right.'

It wasn't only that Angela couldn't hold a pair of scissors properly and couldn't cut. She couldn't add up the simplest things, let alone say her tables. Sometimes Miss Arkwright made them do mental arithmetic round the class, barking out questions which they had to answer immediately. Even when it was not her turn, Angela always put her hand up, waved her hand about, desperate to answer. But she always got the answer wrong. And even when Miss Arkwright made up special sums, specially easy because she knew that Angela had given her the right answer the day before, Angela got the answer wrong. But still she kept on smiling and picking numbers at random out of the air so she could have a go at answering all the questions.

Miss Arkwright was always kind to Angela. And when Angela did jobs for her, watering her plants at lunchtime or collecting her cup of tea at breaktime when she was on gate duty, Aysha went along too. After a few weeks, Miss Arkwright took Aysha aside.

'I've been having a word with the Head of Maths,' she said. 'You're too good for this maths set, Aysha.'

Aysha didn't understand what she was trying to say.

'The maths we do is too easy for you.'

'Yes. It's easy, Miss,' Aysha smiled. 'But it's nice, Miss. I like maths, Miss.'

'Yes, but you're too good. Where did you learn your numbers in English? You're very good at maths, Aysha.'

'I learn in the library, Miss. A lady show me a book there. Bengali numbers. English numbers. Maths is easy, Miss.'

Miss Arkwright leafed through some of the folders on her desk. 'Look, this is the work the others in this group have done. And this is your work. You should be in a higher set.'

'No, Miss! I help Angela, Miss. She help me, Miss.'

Aysha only stayed in the top set for a week. The teacher didn't talk to them and didn't allow them to talk, as they had done in Miss Arkwright's lessons. Every day he told them which pages they had to do and then sat down behind his desk while a queue of girls stood in a silent row waiting to ask him questions. But Aysha couldn't read in English. She couldn't read the questions she was supposed to do and she wasn't allowed to wander round and pick up the right idea from what the other girls were doing. The maths was easy, but the problems were written out in pages and pages of English writing, so Aysha went back to Miss Arkwright and back to helping Angela.

'Too hard, Miss,' she smiled, as she sat down next to her friend.

In Home Economics, they learned about different

kinds of food shops and went out in a long line down the High Street with two teachers instead of the one they usually had. Aysha liked going out. Angela was always her partner and when they went out they could talk as much as they liked, while Angela told her the names of everything she saw. They went to the market and to two supermarkets. And finally, the week before the Christmas holidays, they went on the Underground all the way to Harrods. Aysha took a letter home saying that parents could come if they wanted to. But Aysha's mother said that Aba wouldn't like her going all the way up to town. And in the end nobody else's parents came either.

Angela stood up on the Underground and gave her seat to a fat old man who was panting for breath. Aysha stood up too, and let his wife sit down.

'My, you're a big girl,' said the old man, as soon as he had got his breath back.

Angela grinned proudly. 'My nan says I'm as big as my grandad. But he don't live with her, so I don't know. I've never seen him.'

Then the old man looked at Aysha. 'This ain't your little sister, though, is it?' He winked at them and sat back, placing his hands over his round stomach.

'Nah,' said Angela. 'This is my best friend, Aysha. She's the same age as me.'

'Get away,' said the old man. 'How old is youz?'

'Thirteen.'

'Get away!' The old man smiled at Aysha. His red face shone with the sweat of racing down the steps to catch the train.

'Cor, she ain't 'alf small, ain't she? I mean, you're really big and she's really small, like.'

'She comes from Bangladesh.'

The train stopped at Mile End and the old man and his wife followed the people getting on and off with their eyes, as if they were watching a gripping film on television. As soon as the train started off again, they turned back to talk to Angela.

'Where's youz lot going, then?' The old man nodded towards the other girls and the teachers, spread around the two carriages. Only Angela and Aysha were standing up. 'Ain't yer going up Bethnal Green Museum?'

'Nah,' said Angela proudly, 'we're going up 'Arrods.'

'Up 'Arrods?' The old man dug his old wife in the ribs and winked and chuckled. 'Youz don't know where 'Arrods is, youz lot.'

'Oh yes, I do.' Angela hitched her bag up over her shoulder. She was the only one who had brought her proper schoolbag and all the books she wasn't going to need that day. Then she twirled round the pole she had been holding on to to keep her balance and almost fell over Miss Pearl's feet. She swung back and steadied herself on the pole again, her face shining pink as a tea-rose soap.

''Course I know where 'Arrods is. It's in London.'

The laughter in the carriage battered Aysha's ears, clattering against the rattling noise of the rickety District Line trains. She kept on looking at Angela, afraid that her friend would notice how much the other girls and all the other people in the carriage were laughing at her, afraid that Angela would be hurt and upset. Aysha had no idea why the others were laughing at

Angela, but she heard the cruel laughter and she didn't want anyone, anything, to hurt her friend.

But it was all right. Angela was laughing too, still too excited about their trip to notice what the other girls thought of her. She had never left the East End of London in her life before.

By the time they got off the train to change at South Kensington, the fat old man had finally got his breath back. 'Give my regards to Mr 'Arrod,' he shouted, and the people still left in the carriage burst out laughing again.

'And ask Mrs 'Arrod when she's going to 'ave me round for tea,' they heard him say, as Miss Pearl counted them and the automatic doors rattled and groaned and closed.

Harrods, when they got there, was all too much. Miss Pearl told them to stay with a partner until they met up to go home, and Aysha rushed to stand with Angela.

There were too many people. Just before Christmas, the shoppers, men and women and children, were hung about like Christmas trees with big, thick coats and parcels and Harrods bags and handbags on their hands and rolls of wrapping paper and scarves under their arms and receipts and credit cards held between their teeth. Every time she moved, Aysha bumped into a parcel, usually one with at least four sharp corners. She learned to say, 'Sorry!' and still people glared at her and said ugly things she didn't understand.

There were too many saleswomen, running round Aysha and Angela with their, 'Can I help you?' and

73

making them feel they ought to buy, when neither of them had any money and wouldn't have known where to start buying even if someone had given them a hundred pounds. There were too many beautiful things to buy, too many dresses, too many toys, too many kinds of cups and plates and glasses. Aysha heard Angela say over and over again as she looked at price tags, 'Cor, people must be mad. Must have more money than sense.' And when Angela showed her a wonderful embroidered silk bedspread from India that cost £1,000, Aysha, too, smiled and said, 'Mad!'

'Hey! We're supposed to answer all these questions,' Angela said, all of a sudden, when they got to the television and hi-fi department. 'I know they're about food. But I can't read everything here. How does she expect us to do them?' Angela had already told Aysha why she couldn't read. 'I can read some words,' she said, 'only I had to keep moving schools, so I never learnt much.'

Aysha could read fluently in Bengali and Arabic and since they had found the library she had read nearly all of their two shelves full of books in Bengali. But she still hadn't learned the alphabet in English.

It was Angela's idea to go and look for Miss Pearl and ask her to help them with the worksheet. They passed through the Perfume Hall and saw Shahanara and her friends getting the saleswomen to spray them for free with a different perfume on each wrist. 'Phew!' Angela held her nose and pulled at Aysha's hand, dragging her as fast as she could towards the door which led to the Food Halls.

Aysha felt guilty about being in the Perfume Hall.

74

She thought of her grandfather. She knew he would have liked the store. He would have said, 'This is modern life! Jamdher is old-fashioned! Look at this modern place!' But she remembered, too, how often Dada said that a good Muslim woman shouldn't wear perfume because then men would think she was bad. Aysha's grandmother used to tell them a story about a rich man's wife who was carried off by evil spirits just because she wore perfume. Aysha knew that Dada wouldn't have liked Shahanara, with her perfume and her short skirts and the pretty pink lipstick she always wore. He would have said she was too much like an English girl.

But Aysha was sure her grandfather would like Angela, even if she was an English girl. Sometimes part of her homesickness, the feeling that stole up on her like a cat and landed on her back and weighed her down for a day until she shook it off, was the way she could no longer do quite ordinary things like talking to her grandparents. All her life, her grandparents had never been more than a couple of rooms away, or ten minutes' walk when she wanted to tell them something she had been doing at school. Now, when she wanted to tell them about Angela, her best friend and the kindest person in the whole of England, they were a million miles away. Sometimes she daydreamed of grabbing Angela's hand and saying, 'Come on. My grandad's come to meet you.' She dreamed of the smile on Dada's face when he and Angela finally met.

In one of the Food Halls they stopped to look at the waterfall cascading over a big red fish which was twisted round in a half-moon at the centre of a circle of lobsters and plaice.

'They had fish like that in the market near Jamdher,' Aysha said. Dada had only ever taken Aysha to the fish market once because women and girls didn't usually go there. But she had never forgotten the baskets and baskets of fish and the shouting men and the argument Dada had had with the man who tried to sell them one of his big red fish. He said that the man was asking far too much for the fish and the man had shouted something after them. Dadi was frightened when they told her. She said Aysha's grandfather was a silly old man for arguing and some of the travellers who sold fish were bound to put a curse on him. And the next day, when she found some of her rice was mouldy she said that proved that the man had put a curse on her house. Dada had laughed and said she was a silly old woman for believing such stories. Seeing the large red fish there at Christmas time in England almost made Aysha cry. Angela put her arm round Aysha's shoulders. 'I bet you miss your nan and grandad,' she said.

On the way home, while Angela stood up to let Miss Pearl sit down, Aysha kept her seat, squashed in between Shahanara and a teacher she didn't know. It was the first time Shahanara had ever spoken to her.

Shahanara's lips were the pink of a plastic cyclamen and she pouted in Angela's direction, without exactly looking at Aysha's friend.

'Why do you hang around with her? She's really thick.'

Shahanara made the word 'her' sound like a cockroach or a worm, some slimy, scary creature that you want to get as far away from as you can. The Bengali she spoke was the sort Aysha read in books, not the Bengali they spoke in Jamdher. But the way Shahanara spoke their language made it sound as if she had only ever learned it out of books, as if it wasn't her mother tongue, but an unpleasant medicine she'd been forced to swallow. Whenever she spoke Bengali, she spoke quietly, as if she were ashamed to let anyone hear her.

Aysha looked at Angela. She couldn't understand why Shahanara hadn't used English to say such cruel things about her friend. Shahanara didn't have the right to speak Bengali – not to speak like that, not to slowly pour out words like drops of poison while Angela stood holding on to the hanging strap, smiling at them. The English spoken by the girls in Aysha's class was a language so full of bad words that Angela was always warning her, 'You'd better not say that in front of a teacher. You'd better not learn that word. You'll get in trouble if you use that word.' Aysha wouldn't have been surprised if Shahanara had said bad things about Angela in English. She turned away, but Shahanara persisted, in her strange English accent, using her mother's language to pour out poison.

'You don't have to worry about her. She doesn't understand a word we're saying.'

Shahanara smiled at Angela and kept on smiling in her direction as she said, 'She's so stupid, she wouldn't understand even if we were speaking English.' Angela smiled back at them.

'Why do you keep on being her friend? She's really thick. She's one of the stupidest girls in our year.' Shahanara tossed her head and her beautiful, black curls whipped the side of Aysha's face. 'People are going to start saying you're stupid as well, you know, if you hang around with her.'

Then she smiled her brilliant, white-toothed smile. 'I'm only telling you this for your own good, you know. I want to be nice to you. People already think you're stupid because you don't speak much English and you can't read and write. You don't have to make it worse by going around with her. People are going to think you're just the same.'

'I'd rather be like Angela,' Aysha said. 'I'd rather be like her than like you.' Then she stood up and stood next to Angela. She couldn't reach the hanging strap, so she clung to the side of one of the seats. Her face was burning and her head ached. She didn't look at Angela and she didn't look back at Shahanara. She was scared that she might have done something wrong. Perhaps it would be better to try and be friends with Shahanara. She was the cleverest girl in the class, and beautiful too. Everyone listened to Shahanara. Everyone did what she said.

But that was the problem. Aysha had had enough of doing what someone else thought she should do. Having to move to England was bad enough, having to live in two different hotels in three months and having to leave their room every day and walk around in the snow. No one had asked her whether she wanted to go to England. No one had asked her where she wanted to live. But at least she wanted to make up her own mind about her friends.

*

78

Aysha made a Christmas card for Angela, because all the other girls were giving each other cards. Every day they counted how many they had received and Shahanara always had the most. But Aysha's picture of a Christmas tree, copied from a book, was the only card Angela got. Angela bought Aysha a white teddy bear. Then, on the last day before the holidays, she told Aysha she wasn't coming back any more.

'I've got to go and live with my nan,' she said. Then she started crying.

Aysha didn't know what to say, not in English. She felt angry, angry that anyone should make Angela cry. And she was angry again at the way things kept happening that were beyond her control. She wanted to stop them – whoever the people were who were making Angela go away, because she knew what it felt like. Aysha knew better than anyone what it means to be told you've got to move on, away from your friends, away from the house you've always lived in.

'It's not that bad.' Angela never had a hanky, but Aysha knew where Miss Arkwright kept her box of paper tissues, at the back of the maths cupboard. She pressed one into Angela's hand. 'I love my nan.' Angela squeezed the sodden paper hanky hard against her red-rimmed eyes and still the tears rolled down her reddened cheeks and still her shoulders heaved with the sobs which choked at her words. 'But they've taken my mum away.'

Shahanara was there because their class had all their lessons together, not in sets, on the last day of term. She came and sat beside Angela and shooed the other girls away as they crowded round. 'Better get the stuff out,' she said. 'Miss Arkwright'll be furious.'

'Not if it's the last day,' someone groaned. 'Angela's upset.'

'Miss Arkwright won't care what day it is,' Shahanara said. Then she put her arm round Angela. 'It'll be all right,' she said, 'your mum'll come back to you.' She stroked Angela's damp blonde hair. 'We're all going to miss you, Angela. Honest.'

At the end of the day, Angela tried to find out Aysha's address. 'I can come and visit you,' she said. But Aysha had never seen any visitors at the Eastern Promise Motel. She was sure they wouldn't be allowed. Then Angela got Shahanara to write her nan's address for Aysha, on a piece of Miss Arkwright's paper.

Aysha couldn't read what was on the paper and Angela disappeared. Like Zahida in the bed and breakfast hotel they had lived in, like the ghostly old woman who had peeped out of her window across the road from Faruk's house, like Dadi thousands of miles away in Jamdher, like all the people, all the life Aysha had ever known, Angela faded away to some distant place that had nothing to do with Aysha any more.

And all Aysha had left was the piece of paper, scrawled with an address she couldn't read.

Chapter Eight

The house in Bengal Drive was cold and the carpet on the floor was grey, with massive patterns of sailing ships in a dirty, darker grey that was crazed with waves of dirt enough to make you seasick. The walls were a greasy beige. The water that came out of the taps was freezing and always started off brown or grey, so that the woman from the council who took them to the house said, 'Ooh. I don't like the look of that. Perhaps you'd better stay at the motel a bit before you move in – until they get this water sorted out.'

But Aysha and her mother didn't want to wait. They'd been in England for nearly five months and the house in Bengal Drive was their first real home. There was a gas cooker in the kitchen, buckled on bandy legs and bumped and crooked on all sides like an arthritic old lady, but it was a real gas cooker. There was a table topped with red formica, chipped and ripped by blunt knives and stippled by years of forks waiting for food. But it was the first table they had had all to themselves since they got to England. The stools in the kitchen had ripped plastic seats but there was a soft, lumpy sofa and an armchair in the living-room. Upstairs there was a double bed in one of the rooms. The woman from the council promised she would get hold of another bed for them as soon as she could and asked them if they minded Aysha sleeping on the sofa for a while.

She told them the house was called temporary accommodation – just until the housing office found them a proper place to live. But it felt like a palace. The house in Bengal Drive was the first place in England where they could live as they wanted to live, with no one else telling them what to do.

Aysha's parents spent every spare moment scrubbing and scraping the walls and floors until they finally felt they were clean enough. Faruk arrived one night with their pots and pans and a gift of enough meat and lentils and rice to make a feast. Aysha's father said it wouldn't matter if she missed the first day back at school after the holidays. 'You can help your mother to cook for tonight,' he said. 'For all our guests. We owe a lot to Faruk and his family.'

Aysha knew how Miss Arkwright would shout if she missed a day at school. But she couldn't disobey her father. And her mother had never had to prepare a celebration meal on her own before. All the cooking Ama had ever done had been in Dadi's kitchen, with Dadi telling her what to do and Piara and all the other aunts helping to carry the huge saucepans of rice. Aysha knew she would have to stay at home and help. But she thought of school all day.

And the day after their party, when Faruk and his family and a stream of Aba's friends from work had come to visit, sitting in the living-room and waiting while Aysha and her mother served them with food to celebrate their new home, and after even more people had come and stayed until after midnight, Aysha was up early, dressed in her grey, silky, shalwar kameez ready to go to school. Her father stopped her as he set off for work. 'Your mother needs help with the clearing up,' he said. 'You'd better stay at home, just for today.'

Aba wasn't happy about Aysha going to school now that they had moved. He was worried about the long way she would have to travel from the house in Bengal Drive to Florence Nightingale School, but he didn't want Ama to go with her. Now that they had a home of their own, he said he didn't want his wife wandering around the streets without a man to look after her. He wanted to forget their time in the motel and the way Ama had found her way around very well on her own and the way she had started to learn some English from the people she met at the library. He wanted to forget that time because he said he would be ashamed if people back home knew that he hadn't been able to look after them properly.

Aysha's father worked very long hours, but they didn't know what he did that made him come home looking weary and much older every week. All they knew was that he had a job in the sewing machine factory. Dadi had always boasted that it was a very, very, good job. Aba left their house at seven o'clock every morning and didn't get home until seven at night. For another week he found excuses to make Aysha stay at home from school. Then he talked about changing schools and finding her one that was nearer to their new house.

But Aysha didn't want to change schools. She didn't want to have to go with her father to a different education office, getting lost on the way and watching him being humiliated by secretaries who knew he could hardly speak English and told him to come back in a week. Aysha wanted to get on with her work at Florence Nightingale School. After two weeks of her pleading with him, Aba gave in and let her go.

Aysha was lost. She had followed her father's instructions and caught the bus and then the underground, but something had gone wrong. The train had shot through the station where she was supposed to get off and at the next station there was an announcement she didn't understand. No one understood.

People all around her said, 'What's happening? What did they say?' as they got off the train. And then Aysha found herself pushed along in a crush of people forcing their way towards the tube exit. Firemen in yellow helmets and policemen pushed their way down the steps and past the crowd, as Aysha was driven along the platform and up the steps. Outside the station three fire engines blocked the view of the road, and Aysha had no idea where she was. All she knew was that she would have to get back to the station her father had told her to go to and they weren't letting anyone into the underground.

By the time she got to school it was after breaktime, and she couldn't explain why she was late or why she had missed school for two weeks. She couldn't explain why they shouldn't keep her in detention, either. She didn't have the words to show them how her mother would be sick with worry, shut up alone in their house all day, waiting for her to get home.

The other girls crowded round the new form teacher who'd started in January, trying to explain. 'She doesn't understand a word of English, Miss. She doesn't know what you're talking about.' Aysha did understand, but she was lost. She couldn't find the words to defend herself.

After that, her father wanted to keep her at home for good. Having to stay for detention meant she had to travel home in the rush hour and there was another bomb scare on the tube, so that Aysha had to get off the train again and wait outside the station for what seemed like hours until police let people back in. It would have been easier to stay at home, helping Ama to shop and cook, but there was only one reason Aysha had come to England, only one reason why her grandfather had pushed her to go when it broke his heart to lose her. Dada had wanted Aysha to go to a good school and to get a proper education. Whenever she felt cold and lonely on the way to school she heard him saying, 'When you're an educated lady, you can marry a man of good education. And you'll both get jobs in Dhaka, working for the government, and you'll live in a big house and then I'll be proud to come and stay with you.'

As far as Aysha was concerned, there was no point in being in England if she didn't go to school. She pleaded with her father until he let her go back. Then she never stopped working. Soon she was moved up into the first set for maths again, and this time Shahanara asked the teacher for permission to sit next to her and read the questions in their books that Aysha couldn't read. And Aysha helped Shahanara with the maths that she found so easy to understand as she slowly linked the English words to what she already knew in Bengali.

One day at the end of January, the school was

suddenly a ship in a fierce storm, still at anchor, but battling against a rough sea of litter and dead leaves. Outside, the wind shrieked and rain rattled on the corrugated-iron roof of the science block. Chip papers and crisp bags, grey dust and black twigs, drink cans, and old rags reared up on waves of wind that broke against the windows. Inside, the high glass windows made up of twenty tiny panes of glass apiece, shivered and chattered and jumped around like first years in the playground.

Everyone said they would probably be sent home at lunchtime. In the playground at break, girls clung to each other, screeching and pulling their coats around them even tighter with every gust of wind. Girls who went home for lunch came back with stories of heavy slates being hurled from the rooftops in the High Street, only just missing babies-in-prams and butchers and postmen delivering to shops. Shahanara and her friends almost didn't make it back in time for the bell. 'We went to get a take-away,' she said, 'and the police weren't letting anyone leave the shop. There were slates falling down on people all along the High Street. And windows just breaking for no reason at all.'

The Headmistress said it wasn't safe to send the girls home after lunchtime. The sky went grey and the wind grew wilder and Aysha remembered the stories she'd heard every year when the cyclones hit Bangladesh. Suddenly she knew that something dreadful was going to happen that day. The other girls were giggling and every few minutes the textiles teacher had to say, 'Now calm down, girls. Don't get excited.' Aysha was scared, too scared to laugh and shriek whenever the windows rattled. The grey sky and the dark clouds told her that something terrible was about to happen. She wanted to cry while the others were laughing and joking because they were sure the school would be closed the next day.

Then suddenly one of the girls shouted, 'Look, Miss!' and even the teacher raced to the window that overlooked the science block. A piece of corrugated-iron, razor sharp, was flying through the air as if it were made of paper. It came to rest on the roof of the hall. The textiles teacher picked up the phone on her desk. 'Calm down, girls. Sit down and don't be silly.' The noise in the room was louder than the wind outside and then it subsided as the girls sat down and stabbed their needles into their fabric. Uzma pricked her finger instead of the fabric and laughed as she showed them the drop of blood. Then the textiles teacher put down the phone.

'Now don't panic, girls,' she said. 'I've just spoken to the caretaker. Everything's under control.' She reached into her drawer and pulled out her packet of cigarettes, her hands shaking. Then she remembered she was still in school and put the packet back.

Uzma raised her finger and pointed to the window again.

'Come on, Uzma. Stop fussing about a little cut finger.' Miss Carey pretended to check her register.

'No. Look, Miss!'

Aysha looked and saw that the whole of the black felt roof on the hall had started to flap. Then it took off, slowly, clumsily, like a giant black crow.

'Goodness me! Thank heavens no one's in the play-ground,' Miss Carey said.

87

And then the fire bell rang and the whole school broke loose from its moorings. Girls streamed out into the playground, whirling in the wind and dodging slates and spears of shattered glass. Miss Carey hesitated, but a fire bell couldn't be ignored. 'Deary me! Deary me! I think you can all go home,' she said. 'Take care, girls. Take care.' And laughing and pushing each other, thrilled to be off home early whatever the danger, Aysha's class rushed outside.

Aysha walked out slowly. She wasn't surprised when she saw her father waiting at the school gates. Aba had come to take her home early because he had something to tell her. Aysha's grandmother was dead. He was going to fly home that day.

'Have you saved the money for us to go home already?' For a second, Aysha thought the terrible news meant she could go home to Jamdher, that at least she could be with her grandfather again. Her father pulled her out of the school yard and shook his head. He had to shout above the wind. 'I have enough for my fare. And I'll bring Dada back with me.'

There really wasn't enough money for Aysha and her mother. Aba had to borrow the money for his ticket from Faruk. And there was news that made everything harder to take. Aba was quiet. He didn't shout. But as he packed his things once again in the new suitcase he had bought for his last visit, he said, 'You'll have to stay at home now, Aysha. For a while. Your mother can't spare you to go to school. Just until I get back.' He and Ama had rushed around buying presents the whole of that stormy afternoon. While Aysha had been sitting in school waiting, knowing that something dreadful was about to happen, her parents had rushed from stall to stall in the market, buying toy cars for her cousins, cigarettes for her uncles, a transistor radio for Piara's husband Aqbar, leaving themselves with no time to remember that Dadi was dead.

Aysha watched her father squashing in the cardboard boxes. He had far more presents than clothes. Ama brought his best, most beautiful prayer cap, the one that Dadi had made for him, and laid it on top of the other clothes.

'It's best if you stay at home,' Aba said. 'Your mother needs you. We can't leave her alone, Aysha. And your school will have to be closed for a week or two, because of the roof.' Then he closed the suitcase and fastened the two leather straps that went round the outside. 'Now that you can speak a bit of English, Ama will need you to help her with the shopping.'

Aysha said nothing. Her father knew how much she hated missing school. And Aysha knew how much her grandmother would have shouted at him for making her stay at home. Piara was the only woman in their village who had gone to High School and Dadi would have made sure Aysha went to High School, too, if they had stayed in Bangladesh. She would never have missed a day of school if her grandmother had been there to watch over them.

But it wasn't right to argue with Aba. All her life, Aysha had been taught that children did what their fathers told them. That was why her life in Bangladesh had been so different. In Bangladesh she had been free. As long as her father was thousands of miles away in England he had been a fabulous, kind man who sent presents and money. And of all the children living in the houses on her grandfather's land, Aysha was his favourite. Dada had never made her do what she didn't want to do.

Aysha stared at the side of her father's face as he opened the suitcase once again and bent over to force in another box of chocolates and sweets for her cousins. She could not bring herself to feel sorry for him because his mother had died. What did he have to do with her beloved grandmother? What right did this strange man have to go to Jamdher to the funeral when he'd hardly been back there in the thirteen years since Aysha was born? She saw the wrinkles on his forehead, the blue veins mapped against his shining brown skin and she thought of all the things she might have shouted at him. She might have told him how Dadi had said she had to go to school, how her grandmother had dried her tears and said the main reason for going to England and leaving everyone she loved behind was to go to school and become a great woman. But she said nothing. She stood and stared at him and wondered who had given this stranger the right to say what she must do.

Aba looked up and smiled. 'I'll be back soon. And maybe I'll be able to bring Dada with me. We've got room for him now they've given us this house. And then he'll be able to walk to school with you every day.'

'He won't like it here.'

Aysha thought of her grandfather proudly walking round in the mango grove behind the houses and then taking every visitor out to feel the weight of the big, spiky jackfruit, the biggest one they had ever grown, which had ripened just before Piara's wedding. She thought of him wading knee-deep in the mud of the paddy fields, with one of her little cousins on his back, his shining, strong, dark-brown face creased with years and years of sun and work and smiles.

She could not think of her grandfather in grey, dirty, cold London where filthy, wet papers flapped and wrapped themselves around your legs and the newest shoes turned grey and greasy overnight. There was too much dirt and sadness in the air. She was sure her grandfather would hate it just as much as she had hated being dragged away from home. But still she hoped that he would come.

Chapter Nine

Aba was away in Bangladesh much longer than he'd said. They'd told him he would lose his job if he wasn't back within three weeks. But four weeks went by and there was still no sign of him.

Faruk and his wife came to visit one afternoon and told them about the floods in Bangladesh. They'd seen it on television. Faruk sat on the edge of their sofa and drank tea, while Aysha's mother stood in the doorway to the kitchen, waiting to run and get them another cup of tea the minute they'd finished their first one.

'There's nothing they can do about it,' Faruk said, 'if the roads to the airport are flooded.' His wife sat and ate biscuits. She looked bigger than Faruk, because he was very skinny and she was round and fat, her long kameez tunic stretched tightly across her stomach. Faruk held out his teacup and Ama moved quickly across the room to fill it up, drawing her white dupatta across her hair as she moved towards him. She was beautiful in her white sari.

'Your father's probably just as worried as you are,' Faruk said. 'He's probably trying to get to Dhaka every day. But there's not that many planes going in or out. Not with the floods.'

Faruk's wife shook her head sadly. 'We have to accept it. It's the will of Allah.' Then she coughed.

And then she took another biscuit. Aysha had bought the biscuits specially, from Amina's All Hours Groceries, so they would have something nice in the house if Dada came back with her father.

'Anyway, you don't have to worry,' Faruk said. 'I told your father I'd look after you. And you don't have to worry about paying me back the air fare immediately, either. We can wait for the money.'

Faruk's wife nodded. 'The prophet Muhammad, peace be upon him, says we should help our brothers when we can,' she said. 'We're happy to help you.' Faruk's wife never looked very happy. She coughed, and wiped the biscuit crumbs away from her mouth with the dupatta.

'My wife is not well at all,' said Faruk. 'She has been to the doctor every day this week.' He stood up to go and his wife heaved herself up out of the sofa. 'But I promised your father I'd make sure you were all right.'

Faruk only came twice while Aba was away. He never let his wife go shopping without him because he said it wasn't right for a woman to be out on her own on the streets of London. But he had his business to take care of. He couldn't go shopping with Aysha and her mother as well.

One day they went down to the market. Ama held on tightly to Aysha's arm. She was afraid to touch the things laid out on the stalls because whenever she looked at the fruit or touched any of the fabrics laid out on tables beside the aisles, the stallholders threw words at her loud and fast, words that she didn't understand. She was frightened by the noise and crowds of people, all pushing each other along in the narrow alleys.

Outside the market, it had been snowing again and the road was a thin black line of grey sludge between pavements. Aysha felt good to be there in the warm market hall with the hissing yellow lights hanging in strings over the stalls piled high with apples and oranges, nuts and cauliflowers, potatoes and carrots.

But Ama was often frightened now, when they left the house. She had never had to go out on her own before she got to England. She had been to the fruit and vegetable market near the village, but that was with Aysha's aunts and uncles, never on her own. Only the beggar women went out on their own.

The market near Jamdher was just as crowded, just as noisy. People pushed their way in between the piles of baskets piled high with mangoes and bananas and coconuts, knocking into each other with their black umbrellas held up to keep out the sun. But in Jamdher, Aysha and her mother had never been alone. The market was a place to enjoy, not a place to be scared of.

There was no ginger. Aysha didn't know the word for ginger in English, but she knew what she was looking for and there wasn't a single piece of ginger anywhere in the market. Aysha's mother kept pointing to all the vegetables she had never seen before and asking, 'What's that?' as if Aysha knew everything there was to know about England now that she could speak a few words of English. But it wasn't just that she didn't know the English words. She had no idea what the vegetables were or what you did with them.

94

'Anything I can do for you, darling?' The man had a shiny, brown apron over his thick grey pullover and jingled the coins in the front pocket of the apron as he rocked backwards and forwards on his heels. Aysha looked at her mother. 'There's no ginger. What else do you want?'

'Here! None of that, darling!' The man was grinning at Aysha, but his voice was rough. 'I bet you're telling her something rotten about me. No speaking Indian round here, right?' Then he winked at Ama. 'Don't believe a word she says, darlin'. She's telling you a pack of lies about me, I'll bet.' He laughed. But Ama didn't smile.

'Hey! Don't your mum speak no English, then?'

Aysha shook her head.

'What's she want to come here for if she don't speak no English? It must be like having a baby instead of a mum if you've got to take her everywhere.'

Aysha did not have the words to explain what her mother was doing in England when she didn't want to be there. She didn't have the words to tell of the places they had been and the life they had lived since they'd left Jamdher. And she didn't want to talk and have to tell about her grandmother dying. Even in Bengali, she didn't have the words to tell the man why her mother was there, so far away from everything they loved. So she just smiled.

'Have you lost your tongue and all?' The man had a red face, with red-purple veins that zigzagged across his cheeks like the cracks in a shattered windscreen. 'Can't you speak no English, either?'

'I can speak. Yes,' Aysha said. 'Bye-bye.'

They left the market with onions and potatoes they'd bought from another vegetable stall, from another grey-haired, red-faced man who nodded at Aysha's mother and said, 'Don't she speak no English?' Then he reached forward and pointed to her sari and said, 'Bit thin that dress she's wearing, isn't it? She'll catch her death in this weather.' And he winked at Aysha and said, 'She'd better not go round showing off that gold chain round her neck. Not round 'ere. They'd pinch the shirt off your back round 'ere.'

Aysha encouraged her mother to button her coat right up to the neck before they reached the last aisle in the market. The man at the first stall had been right. She had begun to treat her mother as if she was a child. But there was no one else to look after her.

They left the market by the grey swing doors, next to the stall where a blonde woman with a powdered white face and a black leather mini skirt sold leather coats and skirts. The hot drinks and snacks caravan just outside the door punched at the cold air with its cloud of steam. It was a long way home, a cold, grey sludge of a walk back to the house in Bengal Drive.

Aysha stopped to look in the window of the newsagent's that sold bus passes. She wanted to tell her mother that they sold magazines in Bengali too. But there wasn't any money for things like that – not until Aba got back home and started back at work again.

Then Aysha turned round and saw her mother just about to call her name. Ama's face crumpled up with pain and a hand, a large, white hand with silver rings like rivets on every finger, clamped her mouth and held back the scream.

'Ama! No!' Aysha whispered. Later, she didn't know why she had failed to scream out loud, why her voice had come out as a whisper, pleading for her mother to be left alone.

The woman was as tall as the top of the news-agent's window, with copper-kettle gleaming metal hair and a dead-white face. One of her huge hands pressed against Ama's mouth, pressing Ama's head hard against her red leather jacket. With the other hand, the woman tugged at the gold chain around Ama's neck. Aysha's mother stared at her, so frightened she was hypnotized, and Aysha stood two yards away, not moving, not knowing what to say.

The street was crowded at the far end, near the High Street. But where they were standing, a couple of yards away from the market, it was empty. In another second, the woman had gone, ripping the gold wedding chain from Ama's neck, disappearing while Aysha rushed to her mother and put her arms around her shoulders.

'But the chain was hidden,' she said. 'How did the woman know you were wearing a gold chain under your coat, Ama? How did she know?' Ama grabbed Aysha's arm and clung to it as if it were the rope she needed to stop herself falling down a steep cliff.

The gas street lamp hissed and spat and a cloud of steam glowed around the light. Aysha took her mother's hand and pushed it into her own pocket, clinging to her mother's cold hand and stroking it to warm the fingers as she pulled Ama along the foggy, gritted pavements towards their house. They were alone. There was no one to look after them. Aysha knew she would have to take care of them both.

There was no one she could talk to about what had happened. The house next door had lights in every room and the stereo they heard every weekend hammered away at the walls of their house. But Aysha didn't know who lived in the neighbouring house on the corner of Bengal Drive. At every window, mirrors instead of curtains looked out on the world outside to stop outsiders looking in. A stuffed tiger peered out over one of the mirrors. Someone had painted the word 'NOWHERE' on the garden path. People left the house early in the morning and got back in a large, mushroom-coloured van late in the evening. But they left so early and came so late that Aysha never saw them.

Ama didn't say anything when they got home. And the only thing she'd said, all the long way, was, 'I am so tired.' Then she went upstairs and lay down, still with her woollen coat buttoned up over her thin white sari with the deep blue border. She never mentioned her gold wedding chain. Aysha didn't want to be alone downstairs in the cold, with the hammering of next-door's music on every wall, so she lay down next to Ama on the big bed. By half past seven, in spite of the cold and the noise, they were both fast asleep.

It was cold outside, February dead of night cold, and there was no moon. But a bright light woke Aysha, a light that flickered and danced on the bedroom wall and made the flowers of frost on the window turn into diamonds that sparkled with red and gold and purple. The sound of a wind roared along the back yards outside, but it was a wind-like sound that Aysha had never heard before.

She sat up straight. Ama was standing near the window, a black shape against the fountain of sparkling light. She didn't move.

'What is it, Ama? Why is it so light outside?' Aysha moved to her mother's side, her bare feet cold on the cold linoleum floor.

Ama turned her head to look at Aysha, but she didn't speak. The light from outside their window shone on her beautiful brown face and Aysha put her fingers gently on the red mark around her mother's neck, where the white woman had wrenched her gold chain away in the nightmare of that afternoon.

'Does it hurt?'

Ama shook her head, but her eyes shone with tears that turned to silver face-paints on her cheeks.

Aysha put her arm round her mother's shoulder, pulled her coat more tightly round her thin sari and drew the dupatta up over Ama's hair. It was all she could do. She didn't know what she could say.

They stood together at the window, staring out at the bright, flickering light as if they were still asleep and dreaming. The strange, wind-like noise broke and fell like waves across the back yards outside. Aysha knew the yards, full of dustbins and rusting old barbecues and rubbish and cats. She knew they were there even though she couldn't see them, and that was all part of the dream. Aysha felt warm and relaxed as they gazed at the flickering light. A wind like that, a warm wind that bathed them in heat and light in this cold, grey city could only be part of a dream.

There was a crash downstairs, down where the kitchen and the toilet near the back door jutted so far out into the back yard that they almost touched the back wall of the houses in the next street down. Aysha left her mother standing near the bedroom window. Downstairs, the window in the toilet had been blown in and broken glass lay all over the floor. And suddenly the heat was intense. The warm wind was a roaring dragon, spitting out flames. Aysha reached for the metal handle of the back door and screamed as the heat of it blistered her hand.

'Aysha? Who's there?'

Her mother came slowly down the stairs, staring into the darkness.

'Aysha? Are you still there?'

Aysha stopped herself crying. She wiped her eyes on the sleeve of her anorak and rushed along the passage to keep her mother away from the back of the house. Then she put her left hand through her mother's arm and pulled Ama towards the front door, speaking calmly, as if to a small child she wanted to stay calm.

'We have to go out, Ama. We can't stay here. There's a fire.'

And Ama let herself be led outside.

There was no fire in their house. There was no fire the whole length of their street. But the street was full of people standing at their front gates, talking to neighbours they'd never spoken to in years.

'You wouldn't catch me out the back there. It's enough to singe your eyebrows off,' a man in a black beret was shouting to a woman across the road. 'The windows along our backs are all blown in. My wife was standing there looking out and I told her not to be such an old fool. That's why we come out here. And two minutes later, the back bedroom window . . . Right where she was standing. The back bedroom window was all blown in.' Aysha couldn't see the man's wife. And she could only just see his silhouette. He had glasses on, and a beard jutted out below his black hat.

A woman from the house next door leaned over the hedge.

'Are you all right, love? It's right behind you. Any damage?'

Aysha smiled. 'Yes. All right.'

The woman's hands were shaking. She rolled a thin cigarette, lit it and then took a deep breath of the smoke, as if the smoke in the air wasn't enough. 'My boyfriend's gone round to have a look.'

Then a man ran up the street. He had a pony tail and swung himself in at the gate where the woman still dragged at her cigarette. He pulled it out of her mouth and breathed in and out with the thin cigarette between his own lips, still out of breath from running round the block to the street just behind theirs.

'The bastards!' He spat the cigarette out on to the floor. 'It's that house where the Tamils were living. Petrol bomb through the letter box. There were seven men in there, all asleep. They won't find anyone alive.' He squashed the cigarette with his foot and stamped on it over and over again. 'The poor bastards didn't stand a chance.'

When the woman from the council came the next day to see if they were all right, Aysha's mother had her dupatta draped round her neck, to cover the red mark she wore where her chain had been. 'It's nice to see your pretty hair for a change,' the social worker said, 'I wish I had such lovely black hair.' Her sandy hair was twisted into a plait, with bits that stuck out all over the place, like hanks of unwoven jute.

Aysha wasn't sure if they should tell the social worker about the necklace. The man in the market had warned her mother not to show she was wearing a gold chain. So perhaps he was right. Perhaps they had been stupid. And the necklace was gone now. There was nothing they could do about it.

'Are you both all right?' the woman said. 'I mean, after the fire and everything.'

'Yes,' said Aysha, 'we're all right.' She turned her hand over so Miss Snow wouldn't see it, cooling her blisters on the shiny plastic of the chair.

'I wish I could speak Bengali,' Miss Snow smiled. 'I bet you could tell me all about the fire in Bengali. You must have seen everything.' She patted Aysha's hand, forcing the blisters against the arm of the chair where Aysha was sitting.

'Right, ladies. I'm going to be keeping an eye on you both from now on. What happened last night was definitely a racist attack, and we don't want any more of those. Listen. I'll make sure someone comes round straight away to fix that back window. Can you tell Mum? Can you make her understand? We don't want to leave you alone at a time like this, do we, ladies?'

They didn't see Miss Snow again. And no one ever came to fix the window. Aysha swept up the broken glass and put some cardboard in to cover the hole.

The day after the fire, after Miss Snow had gone, she went out into the back yard. Broken glass and thin flakes of a ragged, black, silk-like material were scattered over everything. The yard was freezing. Aysha stared at the blackened window frames and then at the one unscorched patch of white, flowered bedroom wallpaper. And it was the white of the wall in that burnt out, broken house that touched her and made her cry for the seven men who died.

After that, Aysha didn't go out into the yard any more. And she closed the curtains at the back window of the bedroom.

A week after the fire, Aysha was woken again in the middle of the night by fists banging hard on their front door, voices shouting through their letter box, the sound of car doors banging and voices buzzing or barking instructions on a telephone. This time, there were lights flashing across the front bedroom window, but they were hard, white lights.

'Don't open the door,' Ama said. 'We're alone. Don't open the door.'

Aysha stood behind the curtain, trying to peep out. Three police cars had parked in the road in front of the house. Another car drove up while they were watching, blocking the road so that no other cars could have driven down the road, if anyone had wanted to at two o'clock in the morning. Ama stood behind Aysha, hiding. Lights went on at windows up and down the street. Windows were pushed up and men leaned out to shout. 'What's up? Another fire?'

The banging on the door stopped. Aysha put her arm round her mother and they went and sat down on the bed. It sounded as if the police were going to move on.

'This must be the wrong house,' Aysha said. 'We haven't done anything wrong.' It was deadly silent. A blue flashing light orbited around the bedroom walls and Aysha took another look out of the window. She saw a group of policemen crowded round one of the cars. It looked as if they were all bending over to look at a map. Then they jumped up and ran towards the gate of Aysha's house. And the thumping and crashing against the front door started again.

Aysha didn't want to open the door. But it sounded as if they were going to break the door down. She had to keep them away from her mother, stop them from coming upstairs. Ama was shivering in spite of the coat and the blankets Aysha had slipped around her shoulders.

Aysha slipped away and went quietly down the stairs. She heard each one creak, cold under her bare feet, in spite of the loud voices outside and the fists hammering hard against her front door. As she got to the bottom of the stairs the noises stopped again. But she had to open the door. She had to look outside now and find out what was really going on. So she walked slowly down the hall and pushed the catch down and opened the door, very slowly.

A crowd of faces, tall men with white faces, stared down at her. A man in a leather jacket had his back turned to her, just about to put his shoulder to the door and break it down. He stepped back, and a policeman behind him said, 'Oh. Sorry to disturb you, love. Is Dad at home?'

Aysha shook her head.

'Mum in?'

'She's asleep.'

The policeman nodded his head. He was an old man.

'Well, can you just show us your passport, love? I know it's late . . .'

'Passport?'

'The paper you had when you came to England. With a photo on it. Pass. Port.' The policeman raised his voice and spoke slowly as if Aysha were having to lip-read.

'My passport's in Bangladesh. My dad's in Bangladesh and my name's on his passport. My mum's name on too.'

'Any idea when he'll be back?'

The other policemen started to walk slowly back to their cars and Aysha heard the engines start up.

'Sorry?'

'When's Dad coming home?'

'I don't know,' Aysha said. 'No aeroplanes.'

'All right, love. Sorry to disturb you. Glad we didn't wake Mum.'

Aysha watched him walking down the path. Then she turned and saw the neighbours watching her. She didn't know why the police had come. She didn't know what they had done wrong.

At the top of the stairs Ama was waiting for her, holding on to the banisters.

'We haven't done anything wrong,' she said. 'We've never done anything wrong. The police never came to Dadi's house. They never ever came to Jamdher. The soldiers came, but that was the war. I never saw

105

a policeman when I was as young as you are. Never. What sort of a place is this your father has brought us to?'

It was the first time Aysha had heard her mother say anything against her father.

Chapter Ten

Two days after the police raid, Faruk and his wife arrived with two huge boxes of food.

'I promised your father I'd look after you,' Faruk said. Ama was pleased to see him, but he refused the cup of tea she wanted to make. 'Don't worry about tea,' he said. 'My wife will help you to cook. I'm off to the airport to fetch your husband. And he's got the old man with him.'

Faruk's wife, Anwara, was a wonderful cook, better even than Dadi had been. She didn't waste a minute. Her cooking pots were at the bottom of one of the boxes and she backed into the kitchen, dragging one of the boxes down the corridor and grumbling every time it got stuck in one of the holes in the shiny green lino.

'You can do my spices for me,' she said to Aysha, 'and make me a cup of tea.' She moved quickly when she was cooking, chopping onions so fast that Aysha was scared her fat fingers would fall off.

Ama went upstairs. And when she came down again she had changed. She hadn't changed her clothes, but her face had changed. She pulled Aysha into the living-room. 'We won't tell Aba about the bad things,' she whispered. 'He doesn't need to know about the police or . . .'

'But he'll see there was a fire!'

107

'It doesn't look so bad now.' Ama went down on her knees, sweeping the carpet with the stiff brush they had bought at the market.

'What about your chain?'

Ama put her hand to her throat. She had on another of her beautiful necklaces and the red mark where the woman had ripped the chain from her neck had disappeared.

'I'll tell him. But not now, Aysha! Dada's coming! We've got to make the house beautiful for him. He mustn't think we're poor. And you've got to make yourself beautiful for your grandfather. Let me do your hair.'

Anwara's face was red and dotted with tiny sequins of sweat. She threw open the back door to let in the brisk, no-nonsense March air.

'I've got something for Aysha's hair,' she shouted. 'In the second box. It's my present to Aysha because her grandfather's coming.'

The black scarf was covered with sequins and beads that hung down on gold threads. There was a fringe of gold all around it.

'It's beautiful,' Ama said. 'But Aysha doesn't usually cover her head with the dupatta at home . . .'

'Well, she should do,' Anwara said. 'She's old enough.' She sat down at the kitchen table and started to peel the fresh, knobbly roots of ginger. 'How old are you?'

'Thirteen.' Aysha pulled the scarf forward and folded the sides so that the front of the scarf lay flat on her forehead. Then she tied it under her chin so that none of her hair could be seen. Ama laughed. 'She looks far too old with that on. And she's not going to the Q'ran school. It's her grandfather coming, not the mullah.'

Anwara was the only woman Aysha knew who wore her scarf all the time so that it covered her hair. But then, Anwara was very religious. She had even been on the Haj, the pilgrimage to Mecca.

'Well, she's old enough to be taught to be modest in front of her grandfather. That's what I think.'

For two hours, Anwara chopped and fried and stirred, not even stopping to drink the cups of tea that Ama gave her. And then the smells of ginger and chillies and onions and gharam masala danced around the kitchen, along the hall and right to the front door to welcome their visitors.

'Oh, what a wonderful cook you are, Anwara.' Ama started to set bowls out on the table and Anwara pursed her lips. 'Not as good as my mother,' she said. She had brought everything they needed for a feast – even the coloured powders she let Aysha use to decorate the rice so the biryani changed its patterns like a kaleidoscope every time they stirred it. Suddenly, Ama rushed to the living-room window.

'Here they are. At last! Here they are.'

Ama ran to open the door, but Aysha stayed where she was, in the kitchen with Anwara. She was scared.

She had changed. She knew she had changed since they left Bangladesh in the summer. She was scared that her grandfather wouldn't know her. She untied the scarf Anwara had brought and let it fall on her shoulders. Then she went into the front room and stood at the window, behind the curtain, watching as Faruk opened the boot and began to take out suitcases and plastic bags. Aysha's father got out slowly and reached back inside to the back of the car. Then he pulled out another plastic bag and slammed the door. There was something wrong.

Aysha saw her mother run to the gate and saw her father shake his head and she knew her grandfather wasn't there.

He had been coughing on the plane. 'He's had a cough for weeks,' Aba said. 'Just a cough. It was the immigration people. They say he can't stay in England with a cough like that. They've put him in a hospital near the airport and if he doesn't get better in three weeks they'll send him back. Like a dog. They keep dogs in hospitals near the airport too. Did you know that?' He sat back on the sofa, holding the sheaf of letters in brown envelopes that had come for him while he was away.

Ama began to cry. Anwara started to serve out the biryani and Faruk took the first plateful. 'It's only a cough,' he said. 'I saw the old man before they took him away. He was in good spirits. We'll have him home here in a day or two. And you can go and visit him any time you like.'

'It's a long way,' Aba said, 'to the hospital near the airport. It's taken us more than two hours to get here.'

'You'll just have to cook him good food and take it to him, to help him get better,' Anwara said. 'He won't get better unless he eats. And he won't get anything he likes to eat in an English hospital, that's for sure.'

Chapter Eleven

The rain swept across the shining black school yard in all directions, as if massive windscreen wipers somewhere up in the sky were scooping up all the water there was and dropping it right on to the yard of Aysha's new school. She still had the uniform for Florence Nightingale School, but they wouldn't let her go there any more. They said she had lost her place because she had been away for so long. Then they sent her back to the Education Office.

It was Aysha's grandfather who finally persuaded her father she should go back to school. While he was still in the hospital near the airport he asked them every day what she had learned. And every day they had to remind him that she hadn't been able to go to school because then her mother would have been left alone and Aba didn't want her to be all alone while he was away finding out about work. Dada had shouted at Aysha's father, so loudly that he began to cough all over again and the nurses all came running and told him to calm himself. But Aysha's grandfather wouldn't calm down.

'What did she come to England for then, if she isn't going to learn anything? What did you take her away from her grandmother for, if she isn't going to get an education and be a great woman?'

Aba could only stand by the side of Dada's bed

looking embarrassed and scared. But by the time Dada came out of hospital and came to live with them in the house in Bengal Drive, he had fixed up a new school. For now, at least, Aysha's father had plenty of time to go to the Education Office and see all the people he had to see. He had been away in Bangladesh for so long that they had thrown him out of his job.

On the morning of Aysha's first day, her father wanted to take her to school and talk to her teachers, but Dada was waiting beside the front door. 'I'm going to make sure it's a good school this time,' he said. 'Otherwise, why did she come all this way to England?'

'I've told you why they had to come,' Aba said. 'In England I had a good job. I wanted to make a good life for Aysha and her mother.'

Dada didn't say anything. He just raised his eyes and looked at the ceiling in the hall, where the old green paint was crazed and cracked and dirty. Then he kicked with his sandal against the holes in the shiny green linoleum. 'My Aysha should at least have a good school,' he said. 'You've taken the cleverest of all my grandchildren away from me.'

Ama had made them take an umbrella, but it didn't cover them both. And the wind and the driving rain threw dirty water down their necks, inside Aysha's shoes and over the longer part of her kameez that came down below her coat. They didn't have far to go – along Kimberley Drive, straight down and then across Pretoria Road and into Rhodesia Crescent.

Rhodesia School had high, red-brick walls all around the playground. On top of the walls there

112

were sharp green metal stakes, curved and split at the point, like barbed fish hooks.

It was not quite nine. Aysha was glad the playground was empty. To keep off the rain, Dada had one of Ama's flowered scarves wrapped around his shoulders and over the little crocheted cap he wore on his head. Aysha was afraid the other children would laugh at him. The playground was huge, and blocks of the school were scattered all around it. The rain made great lakes out of hollows where the sun had melted the black tar years and sunny years before and water gushed and struggled round grids choked up with straws and crisp bags and drink cans. They were soaked to the skin and didn't know where to go.

Then a bell went, a bell as loud as a fire alarm, and hundreds of pupils suddenly appeared, rushing and struggling and splashing their way from one building to another, laughing and swearing and fighting, and waving huge bags that they were using either to hit each other or to stop themselves being hit. For two minutes, the noise of the rain clashed with the noise of nine hundred children moving around from one building to another and Aysha and her grandfather moved backwards and forwards trying to find the right place for their nine o'clock appointment.

'Please. We need the office,' said Aysha. But no one seemed to notice her. A second bell went and suddenly everything went quiet. Then a woman came out of the building nearest to where they were standing in the rain and took them inside to the school office.

'Do you speak English?' The woman twisted her

lips as she spoke to Dada, as if he were deaf. Then she turned to Aysha. 'Does your dad speak English?'

Aysha laughed. 'Yes. He's grandad.'

Of course Dada could speak English. Everyone in Jamdher knew that he could speak English. Everyone knew that he had worked as a seaman living near London years ago. And he'd fought for the English in their army in India. Of course he could speak English. But Dada didn't understand any of the questions the woman asked them. She went off to get someone else and pointed to a seat near the door. 'You Sit There Now. Someone Coming.'

'She speaks a strange sort of English,' Dada said. 'I've never heard anyone speak like that before.'

Then the woman came back, speaking to a man in a turban. She brought him over to where they were sitting. 'This is Aysha,' she said, 'and I thought this was the father.' She dropped her voice to a snarling whisper that everyone could hear. 'It's actually the grandfather, but the fathers are sometimes so old, you never quite know.' Then she smiled brightly. 'Aysha's got no language. That's why I came and got you. This is Mr Singh. I'll leave you with him.'

Mr Singh bent down towards them. '*Tumar nam ki?*'

Aysha laughed. '*Amar nam Aysha*. My name's Aysha. She just told you what my name is.'

Mr Singh couldn't say anything else in Bengali. He taught Business Studies and Maths at the school and spoke Punjabi at home. 'That's a highly educated man,' Dada whispered. 'I hope you have him for your teacher. A highly educated man.' Then Mr Singh told Dada he could go. He went into the office to ask

114

what class he should take her to and Aysha watched her grandfather pick his way around the puddles in the yard until he got to the gate, a small, thin figure with the flowered shawl still wrapped around his head and tied at the back under his arms.

Aysha's grandfather was disappointed when he heard that she didn't have Mr Singh as her maths teacher. Mr Singh only taught the top set and they put her in the bottom set for maths because they said she had language difficulties. For the first week, Aysha had to carry a registration form with her to every lesson. It had her name and address and the name of Florence Nightingale, the school she had been to for a few weeks. It said her mother was a housewife and her father was unemployed. Everything else about her life was wiped out. The form didn't have a space for the school she had been to in Bangladesh. And once again, someone had written the words NO LAN-GUAGE, this time in red, across the top of the form.

The maths teacher was a tiny woman, smaller even than Aysha, with a wrinkled brown face and a short bob of copper-coloured hair. She wore silver shoes. Every day, Miss Murry, who was older than Aysha's mother, older even than Aba, wore the same black mini skirt and silver shoes that curled up in a point at the toe.

'Miss, I can speak English. A little bit,' Aysha said, when she handed her form to Miss Murry at the beginning of her first maths lesson. Then she turned round. At the back of the maths class, busy sharpening pencils and arranging them according to colour in different tubs, was a very tall girl with sandpaper

115

blonde hair. It was Angela. Aysha had kept the piece of paper Angela had given her, with her nan's address, at 22, Pretoria Road. But no one had taught her how to read in English.

In another week, Aysha was moved from the bottom maths set to the middle set. 'I'm not having a girl like that in the bottom set, wasting her time,' Miss Murry said. 'She can already do everything we're doing.' A week later, Aysha was moved to the top set with Mr Singh. And a week after that, Angela was moved into the same form as Aysha for every lesson except maths.

'It's the best school I've ever been to,' Aysha said. Dada walked with her to school every day and she walked home with Angela because Angela's nan lived in the next street down. There were other nice girls in her class as well, Emma and Leyla and Lindsey. 'We all hang around together at break,' Aysha wanted to say when she got home one day. But she didn't know the Bengali words for 'hang around', so she told her mother, 'We're all friends.'

'I hope you keep away from those boys,' Dada said every day when they were walking to school. 'A girl's school would have been better.'

But he didn't need to worry. Angela and Emma and Leyla and Lindsey and Aysha all thought the boys in their class were horrible. 'They mess around too much,' Aysha wanted to say, but she didn't know the Bengali words for 'mess around', so she told her grandfather that the boys didn't work.

'How are they going to get an education?' Dada asked.

116

'They don't want an education,' Aysha said. 'They want to be in the army.'

Dada shook his head.

There was one boy who spoke Bengali in Aysha's class. He was the only boy who wanted to work and he usually sat on his own. And then there was Leyla's cousin.

Abdul was always getting into trouble. He never started things. But he couldn't and wouldn't shut up when the other boys, gangs of white boys in crinkled, crackling shell suits, called him a black bastard. He always fought them because they called him names and asked him why he didn't go back where he came from. And he always got into trouble with the teachers. Leyla didn't approve.

'He shouldn't fight, but he can't help it,' she said. 'His father was killed by the government soldiers, fighting in Mogadishu. He thinks you've got to fight. Always I tell him to not listen to them. His mother tells him to not listen to them. And my mother tells him too. But still he fights. He's not afraid.'

Leyla didn't know where her own father was. She didn't know if he was alive or dead. 'I don't know where my dad is either,' said Angela when they first found out about Leyla and the war in Somalia. 'But I don't miss him, really.' The three of them linked arms and strolled together around the playground. Aysha found herself wishing her father would go missing as well. Life had been so much easier back in Bangladesh, as long as he was not around to tell them what to do.

'Do you miss your country?' Aysha said. 'I do.'

Leyla wrinkled up her nose. 'London's horrible,'

she said. 'But in Somalia there's a war, such bad things happening.' She smiled. 'I'll go back to Somalia when the war is over. And you can come and visit me.'

'I used to miss my old school,' said Angela. 'But I'm glad I came here now. Otherwise I would never have got friends with you two.' Every day they linked arms and walked and talked their way over to the furthest side of the playground, so far away from their classroom and the main entrance to the school that they had to run when the bell went so as not to be late. That was how they missed the big fight.

Turhangir whispered to Aysha in Bengali. 'Tell Leyla her cousin was in a fight. He's in trouble. He beat three of them up. They said bad things about his mother and his father. They said Somalia was a dump full of black filth. So he had a fight with them and beat them up. He's really strong. But I bet they're going to get him.'

The next day, Leyla wasn't at school. Her house was only a short walk from the school, through the back entrance, so Angela and Aysha went to look for her at lunchtime.

The pavement in front of Leyla's house was brittle with broken glass that clinked like coins when they walked on it. An old woman leaned over the gate to the house next door. Angela burst out crying. Every window of Leyla's house was broken and through the broken panes in the front door they could see right along the hall to where the back door was open, banging against the wall.

Aysha went slowly up to the front door. It was a tiny house. She couldn't imagine how they had all

118

fitted in there – Leyla and her mother and two sisters and Abdul with his mother and three brothers.

'I reckon the council's probably found them somewhere else,' the old woman next door said. She picked up a tiny dog and held it up to show Aysha over the fence. 'He was barking a lot, but a dog like this isn't much use. A crowd of big boys they was. With stones and bricks. I kept him inside and closed all my curtains so they wouldn't think I was looking at them. They might have turned on my house next. And I'm only a poor pensioner.'

Angela's eyes were red from crying and she kept wiping her nose on the sleeve of her pink shellsuit. 'Was one of the lads called Darrell Foster?' she said.

'Ooh! I couldn't tell you no names,' the old woman said. Her hair was a sort of salmon pink just like her lacy-knit pullover, as if it had once been red and the colour had washed out over the years. 'But they was big lads. And the language! I don't know what they teach you at school today. And they had them coloured baseball boots on. Funny how I saw their feet mostly. I didn't want to look none of them in the eye. One of them had red hair. I told the police that, when they come. And the reporters. I've had two reporters round already.'

'It was Darrell Foster and that lot,' said Angela. 'They were the ones who were picking on Abdul yesterday and he beat Darrell up. They must have come round here with some of their mates.'

'Ooh! They had dogs too. Them ugly, nasty ones.' The old woman kissed her scrawny little ball of hair on its wet nose. 'I kept him in and locked the door.

119

He was barking that much. Their dogs would have eaten him.'

'Where's Leyla gone?' Aysha said.

'Well.' The old woman let her dog hop down on to the miniature patch of grass. 'There's one of the mothers could speak quite good English. And she just said to the police, "We're not staying here. We might get killed." And so they went off with the police. I don't know where. I didn't have much to do with them, really. Best not to, with people like that gunning for them, if you know what I mean.'

Nobody talked about it much at school. The boys who'd attacked Leyla's house were caught the next day. They had to go to the police station for questioning and wait there till their parents came to collect them. Emma Jones's mother worked as a cleaner down at the police station. She heard that they'd smashed up their cell and Darrell Foster's dad had been put in prison for a night because he attacked a policeman when he came to get Darrell. The boys were suspended for a whole week when they got back to school. But they said they didn't mind. They were always missing school anyway. Then they were allowed back into school as if nothing had happened.

One day, Darrell Foster was off even though all his mates were in school. And that hardly ever happened. But Emma Jones knew why he was off. She knew everything that was happening in the Foster family.

'Hey! Darrell Foster's pit bull's been put down,' she said. 'Serves him right, after what they did to Leyla's house.'

Aysha didn't know what a pit bull was, but Angela

immediately started to draw a fierce dog. 'It's like them dogs I told you about. Like they took round to Leyla's house.'

'Oh no. It's nothing to do with Leyla,' Emma said. 'His pit bull bit him last night, grabbed hold of his arm and right through his sleeve. Pity his dad was there, really. It didn't have time to finish the job off properly.'

Chapter Twelve

Dada smiled at Aysha. But it wasn't a smile that creased his whole face up like the outside of a walnut, a smile that made his eyes dance with the light. It was a smile as weak and laboured as the bleeping sound, the lame, tame sound connected to a pale green light on a screen that signalled that Dada's heart was still beating.

Aysha's grandfather could hardly talk. His loud laugh and his strong voice were strangled to a whisper. 'I'm all right, Aysha. Don't look so sad.' His face was grey and thin and there were tubes on both his arms. Aysha didn't want to go near him, but she went and touched his hand. The fingers tried to squeeze her hand, but Dada could hardly move.

The nurse came in. 'Time's up. We mustn't get the patient too excited. Your two minutes are up, love.'

'I'm all right, Aysha,' Dada whispered.

For six days, he was only allowed to have two visitors a day for two minutes each, so Aysha only saw him every other day. But after the first visit, the day when he'd had his heart attack, he never forgot to ask her about school. And he never forgot to tell Aysha's father, 'She has to go to school, even if I'm not there to take her. That's why you brought her all the way to England.'

On the seventh day, Dada was getting better, so

they moved him out of the Intensive Care ward into a normal ward. After that there was no more quiet for Aysha and her grandfather. She never managed to talk with him on her own again.

Men's Surgical was a long, dark room filled with beds where thirty or forty men were recovering from operations. Some of the men were young, but most of them were very old, like Dada. Their pyjamas were old and faded like their faces and it looked as if no one ever bothered to give them a wash. A lot of the men were fat, their great white bellies thrusting out of pyjamas that didn't quite fit. The men who had only just had an operation were supposed to be behind screens, but there weren't enough screens to go round. Men with drips attached to their noses lay on their backs snoring, with their pyjama jackets unbuttoned to reveal a row of red stitches across their stomachs. One man lay fast asleep on his front, with his bottom up in the air, drowning in a sea of the newspapers he had been reading.

'I thought hospitals were clean places.' Ama pulled her dupatta round her head and then held the front corner over her nose, trying to keep out the smell of years of cabbage for lunch, and sweat, and dust.

'I never thought hospitals in England would be like this.' Aysha's father held on to her arm, as if one of the old men, staring out at them from the rows of beds, was going to leap out and attack her.

'It wasn't so bad where Dada was before. It was clean there,' said Aysha. She hadn't seen much of the room where they had kept him for three weeks in the hospital near the airport. She hadn't been allowed to visit him often. But the room in Intensive Care had

had white walls and the tubes going in and out of Dada's thin arms had certainly looked clean, as if everything had been continuously washed by the strong smell of disinfectant. Aysha drew closer to her father as they walked along the centre aisle of the long room, looking for her grandfather. The dirt of Men's Surgical seemed to go on for ever, rows and rows of sick, faded, grubby old men.

'Hallo, darling,' a man with his pyjama jacket open and a fat chest covered in grey hairs whispered to them. When Aysha didn't answer, he swore at them and carried on swearing louder and louder as they went up the ward.

The paint was peeling off the frame of the next door they went through and the wood was splintered where a monster woodworm had taken great bites out of it. Dada's bed was the second on the left through the door. There was a green curtain drawn round the bed next to him.

Dada smiled and whispered to them. 'He's going,' he said, nodding towards the curtain. 'His wife's in there.'

'Where are the nurses? Who looks after you?' Ama still held her scarf over her mouth. She looked as if she was going to be sick. Everywhere there was the smell of unwashed, unloved, forgotten people. And there were no nurses or doctors to be seen.

Dada shook his head. 'I never thought an English hospital would be like this.' He took hold of Aysha's hand and held on to it, like a baby clutching at some-one's finger.

'You should have seen London when I first came here fifty years ago,' he said. 'It was a beautiful place.

Clean and rich and beautiful. Not now. Take me home.'

But they couldn't take him home. He had to stay in that dirty, foul-smelling ward, full of old men swearing and shouting, for seven weeks.

One day, when they visited him early, he was happy. 'My new doctor speaks Bengali,' he said. 'Very nice. Very posh.'

Ama looked at Aysha. Was he going mad?

'He can't do,' said Aba. 'There aren't any men in this place who speak Bengali.'

'Wait and see.' Dada burst out laughing. 'Wait and see. You can see my doctor tomorrow if you come at lunchtime.'

'You're getting thinner every day,' Doctor Choudhury said, in Bengali. 'Are you eating enough?'

Dada smiled and pointed to the tray next to his bed. There were two plates on the tray. One contained a grey-beige broth, like porridge, and the other was half-full of what looked like mushroom soup. The rest of the soup was slopped around the tray and slowly seeping into the paper napkin wrapped round the cutlery Dada was meant to use.

'Do you like the smell?' Dada said. Then he patted Doctor Choudhury's hand and said, 'But I'll be a good boy and eat it if you join me.' He smiled. 'Come on. You take the first spoonful and then I'll eat some of it.'

Aysha's father stood up and the doctor sat down on the chair beside Dada's bed. She shook her head and wrinkled up her nose at the smell of the luke-warm, greasy soup swimming around the tray. 'All right.' She looked tired and there were deep, dark shadows under her eyes. 'Can you bring some food in for him?' she asked Ama. 'He really ought to eat something.'

Dada started to cough again and couldn't stop and the man in the first bed next to the door started to swear at him. Doctor Choudhury drew the green curtains around Dada's bed, but still the young man next to him shouted and swore at him. 'Shut up. Take your germs back where they came from. Take your family back where they came from. Why can't somebody shut them up? They come over here, with their germs, wanting our hospitals, our jobs. Why don't they go back where they came from.'

Doctor Choudhury pressed her lips together and smiled at them and slowly the wave of coughing fell away. 'That young man is very sick,' she said, 'but he's not a very nice man. I'm sorry. We just have to learn to ignore it.'

Dada fell back on his pillow. 'I don't want you bringing food here,' he said. 'The smell puts me off my food. I don't want to eat here. Take me home.'

But they couldn't take him home. He wanted to go back to Bangladesh, to Piara and his house in Jamdher, to the mango trees and the monsoon rain and the hours he spent talking with his neighbours. And they couldn't even take him back to the house in Bengal Drive.

Aysha had never met a woman doctor. And in England, she had never met anyone who spoke Bengali and had such a good job. She talked to Doctor Choudhury every time they visited and one day she asked, 'Is it hard to be a doctor?'

'Do you go to school every day and do your homework?'

Aysha shook her head. She had only been to school for two weeks since Dada had first been taken ill, the two weeks when everyone had thought he was getting better and Dada had sat on the side of his bed and then walked with Aysha holding him, five steps up the ward and five steps back to his bed every night.

'It's impossible to be a doctor unless you work hard, really hard, every day. But you're a clever girl. If you want to be a doctor you can do it. You just have to work. You're not afraid of hard work, are you?'

'But I can't speak English,' said Aysha. 'Not very much, anyway. They all laugh at me.'

'How old are you?'

'Thirteen.'

Doctor Choudhury smiled. 'Listen. I was fourteen when I came here. I couldn't speak a word of English. But I'd started my science back home. Science was always my favourite subject. I couldn't bear to be left out of things. They put me with the children who couldn't read, just because I couldn't speak English, and they didn't let me do science. So I had to learn to read quickly. I couldn't bear to be left out.'

Aysha was happy. 'It's the same with me. They treat me as if I'm really stupid. Everyone speaks slowly to me and acts as if I can't hear properly.' She was scared that Doctor Choudhury might think she was too big-headed. 'So, do you really think I could be a doctor, then?'

'You'll have to work hard – much harder than you can imagine. Just look what a wreck I am!' Doctor

127

Choudhury had to dash away, past the rows of beds, to the end of the ward and Aysha went slowly over to join her mother and father at her grandfather's bed.

'She's a lovely woman,' Dada said, nodding over to where Doctor Choudhury was talking to a relative at the far end of the ward. 'The kindest, nicest doctor I've ever had.'

'You've not had that many doctors before, Dada.' Aysha sat down on her mother's knee, just to be beside him. 'I never saw you going to a doctor.'

'I never needed to until I got to London. London made me sick. And I had to put up with Doctor Mathews in the hospital near the airport, didn't I? I've seen plenty of doctors. And Doctor Choudhury is the nicest and kindest.'

Aysha had tried to forget the awful day when her father arrived back from Bangladesh and Dada wasn't with him. The months since he had arrived back at their house had been so full of new experiences; Angela and the new school and new friends, learning English, and every evening sitting with Dada talking about school and about their village. She had been so happy that she had almost forgotten the illness he had had when he first arrived in England. His cough had never quite gone away and he seemed much smaller and frailer in London, but she had ignored all that. Nothing had mattered as long as she had her beloved grandfather with her.

'You know what I think?' Dada patted Aysha's hand and winked at her. 'I think Aysha should become a doctor.' He spoke faster as he grew to like the idea more and more. 'Her grandmother was always saying she had to get a good education so she could be a secretary in Dhaka. Why does she have to be a secretary? Why can't she be a doctor?'

Aba shook his head. 'We've got to be realistic,' he said. 'Don't go putting stupid ideas into her head. She can't even speak English yet.'

'I can.' Aysha stood up. 'At school I speak English to everyone.'

Her father looked weary. 'Listen, I can speak English too. I've only managed five or six trips back to Bangladesh in all the eighteen years I've been in England. I should be able to speak English after all that time. But there's English and English. It's just not possible, not when it's not your own language. She might be able to get a machine job, sewing or something, where she doesn't have to speak that much. That's how I got by.'

'But I don't want a machine job.' Aysha moved round to the other side of the bed, so she was close to Dada but far away from her father. 'Doctor Choudhury couldn't speak English when she came to England. I'm going to be a doctor like her.'

'Right,' said her grandfather. 'But you've got to start by going to school every day. Your grandmother wanted you to go to school, like Piara.' He raised himself up on his elbow and smiled and shook his finger at her. 'I don't want to see you here tomorrow or any other day unless you've been to school first.'

Aysha's grandfather died a week later, while she was at school.

Aysha had no idea her father had so many friends. As soon as the news came that her grandfather had died they started arriving, men and women Aysha had only seen once or twice before in the weeks when Dada was there with them. There were very old men, older than Dada, who had known him all those years ago, long before Aysha was born, when he had worked in London near the docks. They had come to visit him when he first arrived and now they had come to say goodbye.

Men from the factory Aysha's father used to work in came and stood outside the house while the women sat on the floor, crying and eating the food which Aysha and her mother and Faruk's wife, Anwara, rushed to prepare.

They brought Dada home to the house in Bengal Drive before they took the coffin to the airport. The men from the funeral service set the coffin on a pedestal on an ornate carpet, blue with yellow scrolled patterns. Aba draped the coffin with a green cloth, pulled back so they could see Dada's face through a small, square-shaped pane of glass. One of the men stood by the coffin and held up toddlers and small children so they could look inside. The women prayed, their heads covered with white shawls, and then stepped back away from the coffin and cried. Most of the men stood outside on the step, in the hall, in the streets, all dressed in their white tunics and trousers, with prayer caps on their heads.

One of their neighbours, an English woman from across the road, knocked at the door. 'Just come to pay my respects, my dear,' she said. She didn't take her shoes off or cover her head with a scarf, and some of the women glared at her. But she shook Ama's hand as she went out. 'He was a nice old man,' she said. 'Always gave me a smile and a wave.'

Aysha watched her father. He didn't cry, but stood talking quietly with the other men. Ama rushed around cooking and serving tea, but she broke down as the coffin, with the green cloth embroidered with gold on top of it, was loaded into the shiny, black English funeral car.

The sun was shining as the black limousine cruised away slowly along their street. Aysha had only ever seen one funeral before, once in Bangladesh. It was during the rains and the dead man was one of the poorest in their village. Her grandmother had told her he died because he didn't get enough to eat. In the driving monsoon rain, Aysha had watched the funeral party creeping silently along a narrow mud track through the rice fields, the man's wife, thin and bony in a white sari that was lashed to her body by the rain, held up on either side by neighbours who were just as poor and miserable.

The sun sparkled on the polished, posh black limousine as it drove away and Aysha knew she had seen Dada for the last time. The sun was warm and shone more brightly than she had ever known it to shine in cold, grey England. And it didn't seem right for the sun to shine as if nothing had happened. Aysha longed for the monsoon rains to come and wash away her tears.

Chapter Thirteen

The cars were packed together as tightly as they would have been on a cross-channel ferry. They had scarcely moved for more than half an hour. When anything happened on Pretoria Road, the main road between Aysha's house and the school, whenever there was an accident or the traffic lights broke down, nobody in a car got to work before ten o'clock.

Aysha decided not to bother walking along to the traffic lights. She didn't have to. But then she saw the man with the tweed jacket, the one she'd noticed every day on her way to school since she'd started going there on her own. He looked lost and scared, even though he was a big man, with huge, red and purple hands. His feet were lost in shiny, polished red-brown shoes, shoes that were knobbly as a sack of potatoes, with lumps and bumps in all the wrong places where his toes couldn't possibly be. He had on a hairy, mustard-coloured Harris tweed jacket and brown cord trousers. And he always looked as if he was trying to fold himself up to hide some of his great height like a scarecrow who had been very neatly dressed before someone decided to use him as a punchbag. The man was older than Aysha's father, but something told her he was still a child. He had crooked teeth and a crooked smile and his steel-rimmed glasses drooped down on the right side of his face so that his right eye peered out over the top of them.

Aysha watched him. He had stopped at the traffic lights as he always did, but the traffic lights weren't working. So he just stood there. He stood for what seemed like ages. Sometimes he looked to the left and sometimes to the right. People wound down their windows and shouted that it was all right for him to cross. Every few minutes, the cars inched forwards and a new car drew up alongside him so the people inside could wave and shout at him or honk their horns. But the man didn't move.

Aysha remembered her first few weeks at school in England, when she had been so scared of saying the wrong thing, making the wrong move, that she couldn't say or do anything. That all seemed a very long time ago. But she could see that the man was scared. The traffic lights were broken and the cars were at a standstill and still he didn't know what to do. Aysha walked back along the road to the traffic lights.

Someone had written the name, BARRY, in black marker pen on the white plastic carrier bag the man was clutching in his left hand. 'You can come with me, Barry,' Aysha said. Barry smiled and nodded and put his hand into her arm and together they walked across the road.

After that, Aysha looked out for him every day. He waited for her at the crossing and she helped him across the road and then waved to him when he turned into a big house on the way to school. She never saw him after school. Angela told her about the house he went to. 'It's for people who can't work

133

properly,' she said. 'So they go in there and make baskets and things. We went to sing for them once at Christmas, from my primary school.' She said there was a minibus to take the people home at night.

Aysha's father finally found a job. He told them it was a good job, with prospects, but Anwara told them what it really was. 'Faruk wanted to do what he could for him,' she said. 'That's what we're here for – to help each other. It's only cleaning for the moment, sweeping round the machines and cleaning the toilets. But it's better than nothing. It's not good for a man to be without a job.'

Faruk had lent Ama one of his sewing machines and she started to work, too, sewing pretty dresses for little girls, pink and blue and yellow satin, with wide skirts and frills and lots of lace. All day and the whole of the evening, whenever Ama wasn't cooking, the sewing machine in their living-room was buzzing like a chainsaw.

So Aysha could do what she wanted. And she wanted to stay on late at school, for the reading classes she knew her mother and father would approve of and for the running club she knew her father would forbid. She wasn't sure what her mother would have to say about the running club, so she didn't ask. She just told them there were extra reading classes every night.

'Your grandfather would have been so proud of you, Aysha, reading in English as well as Bengali.' Her mother held up one of the little dresses, almost finished. 'If we save up enough money, Faruk can get us a television, cheap. I only have to keep sewing these. One day we can see Piara's wedding too.'

Dada had brought them the video film of Piara's wedding. He had asked the photographer to come all the way from Sylhet because someone had told him that everyone in England had a television and a video. Aysha's grandfather had paid a fortune to have a video made of the wedding so they could show it over and over again to their friends in England. But no one had ever seen it.

As it got closer to the end of the school year, the days grew warmer and there were more and more practices for sports day. Aysha had been chosen to run for her class in the girls' 800 metres race. Angela came along to watch every night, but she never wanted to take part. 'I'm too slow,' she said. 'My mum said so.'

'Why don't you enter the three-legged race together?' Miss Turner asked.

'Nah!' Angela went red and tucked her blouse into her navy blue skirt. 'I'm too big for Aysha. We'd fall over.'

'Have a go! It's only for a laugh.'

Miss Turner bound their legs together with a short rope and they started trying to walk and fell over in a giggling heap. Then they walked and fell, walked and fell, until Aysha started to count.

'If I say one, two, three . . . one, two, three and we run together . . . Let's try it.' They walked together. Then they managed to run.

'Wicked! Let's practise.' Angela ran over to Miss Turner. 'It's more than a week till Sports Day, isn't it? So if we practise every night . . .'

Anyone could enter the three-legged race. You didn't have to be chosen to run for your form, but

135

you could win points to help them win the cup. A week before the race, Emma brought some running shoes into school. 'I've grown out of these, Aysha. My mum says you can have them to win your race.' They looked brand new.

Then the Sports Day arrived. There were some parents there, sitting at the far end of the stadium, far away from where the classes were crowded together, eating crisps and drinking fizzy orange. But plenty of people didn't have anyone to watch them. Aysha told Miss Turner her mum and dad were working, which was true.

8S were doing all right. Aysha screamed herself hoarse when Nick won the boys' 100 metres, and Michelle easily won the hurdles. Michelle was the only one in the second year who went to an athletics club – because her dad was in one. Then it was Aysha's turn. Everyone in her class was patting her on the back, smiling. Everyone wanted her to win.

The voices she heard as she walked over to the start of the race were all the voices of her friends, everyone wishing her well. 'Go for it, Aysha. You can win.'

'Aren't you going to take your tracksuit trousers off? It's ever so hot.' Miss Turner held out her hand. 'I'll look after them for you.' But Aysha shook her head. It was bad enough to go to the running club every night. She didn't know what her mother would say if she wore the short shorts the other girls had on.

The race was easy, so easy. After all the training, it was no problem for Aysha to coast through the 800 metres way ahead of the others. Some girls even had to stop and walk, their faces red with exhaustion. And it was wonderful. The whole stadium, parents, pupils, teachers, everyone was on their feet and cheering, shouting Aysha's name. Angela ran out to the finishing line and hugged her. 8S were leaping up and down with excitement. It had all been so easy, as easy as chasing around Jamdher with her cousins. The sports teachers crowded round her.

'You ought to join an athletics club,' Miss Turner said. 'You're a natural runner.'

Aysha smiled. There was no way she could think of to persuade her father to let her run in a club with boys. She knew what he would say. That was why she hadn't asked him. And she knew that it wasn't only her father this time. Faruk's wife, Anwara, had already tried, unsuccessfully, to persuade Aysha's grandfather that she should cover her head all the time and stay at home. And every time Anwara had argued with the old man, she had used the same words. 'She's almost grown up. A grown-up girl can't wander around on her own. A grown-up girl should cover her hair in front of men. Can't you see that she's growing up?'

Aysha knew that even if she had stayed in Jamdher she would soon have been punished with what they called 'being grown up'. She had seen it happen with all the girls. Even if they had never left Bangladesh she would soon have had to stop running around playing football in the fields and climbing trees as fast as her cousins did – because she was growing up and girls were not supposed to do that sort of thing. But Anwara made growing up in England seem even worse. No one Aysha knew in Bangladesh would ever have said she had to cover her hair in front of her own grandfather.

Aysha walked over to the timekeeper's table to give her name to the teachers who were keeping records of who won each race. Then she turned towards the stands and bent down to pull up her sock, wrinkled inside her right shoe. She hadn't noticed it scratching at her foot during the race.

'Your father would be proud of you, Aysha. What a pity he isn't here to see what a good runner you are.'

Mr Gilman's face was pink and shiny in the afternoon sun, his chin nestled on a grey Paisley cravat as if he had no neck. Other teachers wore track-suits or shorts, but Mr Gilman had on his usual grey sports jacket and stiffly pleated grey trousers. Aysha didn't like to look at his face, at his watery blue eyes. His nicotine-stained teeth, his thin lips which shone like the trails left by a slug, his polished jet-black hair, made her feel sick with fear. She didn't know why she felt so afraid of him.

'Does your father know you've been running every night this term?'

Aysha looked up and shook her head and then stared down at the ground again, undoing and retying the laces on both her trainers. Mr Gilman's lips had wrinkled into a smile. She didn't want to look at him.

'Well, you don't have to worry on my account. I know what some of these fathers are like. I certainly shan't tell him.'

He knelt down beside her and the smell of stale tobacco grabbed at Aysha's throat.

'Are you all right, my dear?' Mr Gilman placed his

hand on her cheek and stroked the damp hair away from Aysha's face.

For a second Aysha's whole body froze. Then she jumped up and ran away, smiling. She felt sick. She felt as if she had done something terribly wrong, but she didn't know what she had done.

'I saw that Mr Gilman talking to you,' Angela said. 'He's a creep. Yeuck! And he's a dirty old man an' all. My nan says that every time she sees him in the High Street he's always chatting up all the girls. Yeuck! I'm glad he doesn't teach us.'

Angela and Aysha came second in the three-legged race, behind one of the deputy heads and an art teacher. The whole school laughed and cheered and everyone who took part in the race got a prize, a chocolate egg that melted in the sun and made Aysha feel sick after the first bite. She gave hers away and drank some water and then 8S won the relay race. Cheering them on, happy with all her friends, Aysha forgot about Mr Gilman.

It was the best time Aysha had ever had in England. It was even better than her school in the village, where they didn't have sport and where they sat on hard benches and had to work hard all morning. She walked home with Angela, still laughing over the three-legged race and Angela kept saying, 'Oh, I feel sick. I feel sick. I shouldn't have eaten that egg. Oh, yeuck, I feel sick.' And then they were laughing again about Angela nearly falling over and the Deputy Head swearing as she and her partner ran past them and the rope cut into her legs. And then they linked arms and hopped along the road, as if they were still in the race together, stopping and laughing whenever they had to catch their breath.

And then they saw the fight. Three boys from the third year, three white boys, were hitting out with rounders' bats and swearing, all crowded round someone lying on the floor. Aysha stopped walking. She was scared of them, but Angela ran forward.

'Leave off or I'll get my dad. My dad's a policeman. Leave off.'

'Get running.' It was Darrell Foster. He gave one last kick and ran away. The other two boys had already turned the corner. The boy they had attacked stood up and then sat down again suddenly on the low wall of someone's front garden. It was Turhangir. Suddenly he leaned forward and threw up all over the pavement and then slumped down on the wall, his head down between his knees. Then he put his hands up to his head so that blood ran down his wrists from a deep cut and Angela burst out crying.

'The rotten cowards,' she said. Then she sat down next to Turhangir on the wall and put her arm round his shoulder. 'I never knew they'd run away from me. I was scared stiff, Aysha.'

The front door of the house opened slowly, just a crack, and then a woman came out, followed by four tiny children, who ran back into the house again laughing and then ran out to have another look at the girls.

'I wasn't sure whether I should call the police,' she said. 'I wasn't sure if you'd want me to. If it was just a fight between friends, like. I didn't want to cause no trouble.'

'They had rounders' bats.' Angela wiped her nose

on the edge of her shoe bag and then wiped her eyes on her skirt. 'They were hitting him with rounders' bats. I don't think that was very friendly.'

Turhangir wasn't listening to her. His head hung down and he looked as if he was going to be sick again.

The woman rang for an ambulance and Aysha had to go with Turhangir to the hospital. He didn't answer anyone when they spoke to him in English. Whatever they said to him, he just stared straight ahead. But she got him to nod or shake his head when she asked the doctor's questions in Bengali. Then the police came to the hospital and Aysha told them the names of the three boys and the words they had shouted out as they hit Turhangir over and over again with the rounders' bats.

Turhangir's father and mother came to the hospital. 'I'm sure they didn't mean it,' Turhangir's father said. 'It's just the way boys are sometimes. Boys like fighting. I'm sure we can sort everything out if we just sit down together with the boys' parents and talk it all over. They'll have to recognize that we are human beings as well. I'm sure we can sort it out.'

But Aysha wasn't so sure. She had seen what Darrell and his friends had done to Leyla's house. She had heard what they said in the playground to anyone who wasn't white and English. Turhangir's parents took her home and she had to explain to her own parents what had happened, why she was late. Her father looked grim. 'I should have known this would happen,' he said. 'I shouldn't have brought you here to London.'

In the end, Turhangir's family moved away. The

141

council found them a different house, far away from the Fosters, and Turhangir went to another school. It was the fourth school he had been to and he'd only been in England for eighteen months. Darrell Foster and his friends were finally expelled from Aysha's school, but they still lived in the area and Angela was still scared of them.

'Don't worry,' Aysha said. 'They won't touch you. Your dad's a policeman, remember?'

'Maybe he is.' Angela grinned and then pulled a face. 'For all I know. And anyway, my nan would beat them up if they came anywhere near me.'

Chapter Fourteen

After the sports day was over there were no more practices after school, so for the first time Aysha went to Angela's house. Angela lived with her grandmother close to the Day Centre Aysha passed on her way to school, the house that Barry went into every day after she had helped him across the road. Angela's nan gave them orange squash and chocolate digestives and they watched videos for an hour.

'We've got a video,' Aysha said, 'of my aunty's wedding. But we haven't got a television. We've never seen the video.'

'Why don't you bring it here and watch it?' Angela's nan didn't look very old, nothing like as old as Dada. She had short, cropped, silvery-grey hair and bright red lipstick and she was wearing a huge, baggy T-shirt and Bermuda shorts. She worked at a petrol station while Angela was out at school.

'My mum hasn't seen the video,' Aysha said.

'Well, bring your mum along too.'

Ama was scared of going to an English house. She had never been invited inside an English house the whole time they had been in England and she was still afraid she couldn't speak English well enough. But that was no problem at Angela's house – if you didn't count the fact that Angela's nan treated Ama as if she were a baby.

'Isn't she lovely! Pretty as a picture!' Angela's nan stroked the silky fabric of Ama's deep blue sari.

'Can't she say nothing yet, darling?'

Ama smiled and Angela's nan made her cups and cups of tea and kept urging her to take more biscuits.

The soundtrack on the video warbled and crackled like an aged opera singer.

'Is that your Indian music, like?' Angela's nan said. The camera swooped through the jungle, searching for its victims like a bird of prey, and then took off down to the river.

'That's the river next to Jamdher,' Aysha said. 'On one side of the river it's India and on the other side it's Bangladesh, where we live.'

Angela's nan lit up a cigarette. 'I always thought Bangladesh was in India,' she said. 'You learn something new every day, don't you, darling?'

She nudged Ama on the elbow and Ama smiled and said 'Yes.' Aysha was beginning to get embarrassed. She wondered why her mother didn't try to learn more English. It made her look stupid, not being able to speak English. And Ama wasn't stupid.

The waving, shaking, wobbly music of the soundtrack did a tight-rope dance along the river bank to where a crowd of men were standing. 'They're waiting for Piara's husband,' Aysha said. Then the camera shook and bumped and plunged towards the line of people on the opposite bank of the river. 'Look, lots of people from India came out to see the wedding. It was the best wedding anyone in our village had ever had.'

'Hey, look! That boat's like a double-decker bus.' Angela grabbed another handful of biscuits as they watched the groom walk down the gangplank of the river boat and step into a sort of sedan chair to be carried towards the village. The waiting men heaped paper chains around the neck of his white and silver suit, standing on tiptoe to place the garlands carefully over the white turban he was wearing. The groom put his hands up to readjust his turban and the camera closed in on his face and the jewelled brooch in the turban pinned to a long white plume of feathers.

'My word! He's tasty. Doesn't he look like Omar Sharif!' Angela's nan said. 'I said, he's got a look of Omar Sharif!' she shouted, as if Ama couldn't possibly have heard her the first time.

'They're going to the mosque now. Look! Those are my uncles,' Aysha said. But by the time she had jumped up from the settee to point to her three uncles on the screen, the film had moved on to a view of the white village mosque, its shape picked out in shadows by the sun. Angela's nan pulled the remote control out from under a pile of newspapers.

'Hang on. Let's have another look,' she said, and took the film back to where the men were standing on tiptoe to place the flowered paper garlands round the groom's neck. Aysha pointed to her uncles. Two of them were wearing shirts and the long, cool cotton skirts that all the men wore, called lunghis. But Uncle Ruhul, who worked in Dhaka, wore a navy blue double-breasted sports jacket with gold buttons. Aysha couldn't see her cousin from Dhaka on the film, but he had worn a sports jacket just like his father.

She remembered how she thought he was lovely

and how she'd whispered to Piara that she wanted to marry someone like him. And Piara had told Aysha's grandmother. That was when they'd both told her she would really have to go to England. They said if she went to a good school in England she could be a secretary in Dhaka and then marry a man like her cousin. But Aysha didn't want to be a secretary in Dhaka any more. She wasn't even sure if she wanted to marry someone like her cousin.

'Cor, aren't they lovely?' Angela's nan's shiny red lips puckered round her cigarette and she squinted at the film as she blew out smoke. 'Do they all look like Omar Sharif in your village? I wouldn't mind living there.' Angela put both her hands over her eyes and wrinkled up her face at Aysha.

Ama smiled and nodded. 'Yes,' she said.

Aysha groaned and clutched her forehead and pulled an even worse face back at Angela. She wished she could disappear through a crack in the floor. Or at least teach her mother English, quickly.

After the camera had taken the groom and the other men off to the mosque, the screen was suddenly filled with twenty images of the bride – one in the middle and the other pictures of her shy, made-up face swirling round the centre, like the images in a kaleidoscope. But it was all the same picture of Aysha's aunt. Piara was hardly recognizable in her red sari and with so much make-up. Then the film moved back to the day before the wedding when an old woman from the town had come to do the mehndi patterns on Piara's hands and all the women and children in the village crowded round to watch her painting on the swirling, dancing designs. Aysha saw them walking to the pond where she used to swim with her cousins and watched her aunts walk slowly past, one by one, carrying water back to her grandfather's house. They were so large as the camera moved in for a close-up, but Aysha knew that she couldn't reach out and touch them. There was a whole world between them now, keeping them apart.

Then the camera swooped back to the day of the wedding again and Aysha shrieked, 'Oh no! Oh no!'

'What is it? What's the matter?' Angela's nan, with her finger on the remote control, stopped the film and stood up and stubbed out her cigarette and then whirled round to Aysha again.

'Oh no! Look!' Aysha was laughing, covering her face with her hands. 'Oh, my God! Look at me!'

Angela's nan had stopped the film just at the place where a little girl in a red dress, with her hair in shining black plaits, was pulling a face at the camera. Ama scolded her. 'Look how you spoiled the film, Aysha, pulling a face like that.'

Angela grinned. 'But I thought you said this film was last year – just before you came to England.'

'It was. It was!'

'My God, you've grown,' said Angela's nan. 'You were only a little girl there. Just look how she's grown!' she said to Aysha's mother.

'And I didn't know English then.' Aysha was amazed. 'No English . . . I didn't know no English . . . When they took that film at the wedding . . . I couldn't speak no English when I got here.'

'Well, our Angela must be teaching you proper, then,' said Angela's nan.

Ama told Aysha not to tell her father they'd seen

the film. 'It'd only make him feel bad because we haven't got our own video machine yet,' she said.

There were only two more days of school to go, after they watched the video at Angela's house. The teachers were all so nice, the weather was hot and they had some of their lessons outside, just as Aysha had done in Bangladesh when it wasn't raining. In Jamdher, the benches were hard in the one long room that made up the village school and they still had to write on their knees, so they loved having lessons outside, under a tree. In England it was just as good.

Aysha sat next to her English teacher out on the grass near the gym. No one was doing much work. Miss Edwards had on a very short skirt and her fat knees looked pink and blotchy and freckled, with little lines cut into them where she'd been kneeling on the grass. Aysha looked at her own thin, brown arm and then at Miss Edwards' arm, white and round and purple and pink and flecked with freckles.

'Miss . . .'

'Mm? . . . What, Aysha?' Miss Edwards poked at a piece of green apple peel that had stayed wedged in one of the large gaps between her front teeth since lunchtime.

'Miss, do you like brown colour?'

'Mm? Yes.'

'A brown colour skin, Miss. You like it?'

'I like all colours. Except I don't like mine. I'm too white, so I get burnt when I go in the sun. It's stupid, isn't it? Most people don't like the way they are, do they?'

'Yes ... No ... Miss, I don't know!' Aysha laughed. 'I like my way. I like brown colour skin, Miss. But you're nice too, Miss.'

She didn't dare to tell anyone else, not even Angela, but she didn't want the school term to end. She was happy with her school, happy in England. She knew she wouldn't be able to wait till the holidays were over.

Chapter Fifteen

Aysha was angry and bored. It was hot and stuffy in the house in Bengal Drive in August, but Aba didn't like them going out as long as he was at work. Aysha had stayed at home the whole of the long summer holidays, helping her mother to sew the tiny satin dresses for Faruk's factory. It wasn't that she minded helping. But she couldn't understand why they couldn't go out just for once, why they couldn't sit and do their sewing in the park or take their work to Angela's nan's house. But every time she asked, Ama said the same thing. Aba didn't like them going out without him.

'But we used to go out without him when we lived in the motel,' Aysha said. 'And I go to school on my own. And anyway, he doesn't have to know what we do.'

Ama spoke then as if Aysha had never said anything. 'I met a woman who works in the factory once,' she said. 'When Aba took me to Anwara's house. She says you can earn more money when you go to the factory to sew, but Aba won't let me. We could do with the money.'

'Why don't you just go?' said Aysha. 'You would still get home before he does.'

'Aba wouldn't like it. He says the women all go round talking to men in the factories.'

'So? You wouldn't do anything bad, Ama. You don't have to let him tell you what to do all the time.'

Ama pressed her lips together and snapped the thread off one of the buttons she was sewing. 'You'll see when you get married, Aysha.' She sighed. 'You have to do what your husband tells you to do. It isn't right to disobey.'

She looked sideways at Aysha and spoke quickly. They were both afraid of the angry words Aysha wanted to shout, words she desperately wanted to throw at her father, to make him listen to them.

'Listen, Aysha.' Ama was quiet while she threaded her needle with the pale pink, silky nylon thread.

'Never forget – I've got a good husband and you've got a good father. We always have enough good things to eat . . .'

'That's because you get the good things from the market and then spend hours cooking them.'

'Yes, but I wouldn't be able to cook for us if Aba didn't give us the money to buy food.'

'You're earning money too!' Aysha shouted. She tore at a piece of nylon lace because she had stitched it on too low down, and it would have ended up inside the hem of the dress. 'You work hard! Your money pays for some of the things we eat as well as his.'

Ama didn't say anything for a long time. She bent her head down and threaded the machine up to sew a pile of twenty tiny bodices to skirts. The sewing machine sawed its way through Aysha's brain, backwards and forwards, backwards and forwards. Her mother was very good and very quick at sewing, but the machine made the whole house shake.

151

'He is a good husband, Aysha,' her mother said at long last. The machine buzzed and sawed its way through two more garments.

'At least I can say he's never beaten me. He never laid a finger on you or me, Aysha.'

'What sort of a husband is that?' shouted Aysha. 'Is that all that's good about him, that he didn't beat you? We hardly ever saw him. It was Dada who looked after us. And now he thinks he's got the right to tell us what to do all the time.'

'Aysha, Aysha!' Her mother ripped open the buttonholes she had made, one by one, all down the back of the first little dress, and her words stabbed like the scissors. 'What is happening to you? You're not my little girl any more. You're not the nice little girl you used to be.'

She didn't ask Aysha to help her with the cooking that night. And she didn't call Aysha down from her room when it was time to eat. It was Aba who came to her bedroom door. Everything was different. Everything was wrong.

Usually, Aysha was busy in the kitchen chattering away to her mother when Aba got home from work and sat down in the living-room quietly, chewing at the betel nuts Ama put out ready for him. Usually he stayed in the living-room on his own, because Ama said he needed peace and quiet, until Ama clapped her hands and told him he had to get washed and sit down to eat. But this time Aysha heard him go into the kitchen and shut the door when he got home. And she heard them talking in low voices, Aba raising his voice to shout and then talking quietly again. She couldn't hear a word they were saying, but she knew they were talking about her. And perhaps Ama was telling Aysha's father all the bad things she had said about him.

Aysha didn't care. Why should Ama think a man was a good husband, just because he didn't beat her? That wasn't enough. If that was all there was Aysha didn't want to get married. Why should being married be so special if that was all there was? Many of Aysha's teachers weren't married. And that didn't mean they were poor, sad women like the beggar women she knew in Jamdher whose husbands had died or gone off and left them. Her teachers weren't women you could feel sorry for, like one of Anwara's friends who still lived with her mother because she had no brothers to look for a husband for her. Aysha's teachers had cars and they looked happy in their work. Nobody seemed to feel sorry for them. Maybe women didn't have to get married in England.

'We want to talk to you,' Aba said. Then he turned and went downstairs. By the time Aysha got down, he was already sitting and eating his meal. He made slurping sounds with the rice through his teeth and there were red stains from the betel nut round the edge of his lips. Aysha didn't want anything to eat. Ama sat on the small, low stool at the edge of the table, crying quietly, but ready to go into the kitchen as soon as Aba wanted more rice.

'I've been hearing things about you. From one of your teachers.'

Aysha thought of the Sports Day. Aba had found out about the Sports Day and all the running she had done in the weeks before. She was going to tell him about it, tell him that she had always dressed modestly and trained with the girls, not with the boys. She was going to tell him that the races she had been in were all girls, not boys. It was no good telling him she had won the races. That would only make him more angry. But she was going to tell him that she hadn't done anything wrong when he interrupted her thoughts.

'You've been seen with a man.'

Ama started crying again, wailing out loud, burying her face in her dupatta and crying like a baby.

Aysha didn't know what he was talking about. She couldn't understand why Aba was so angry. 'You're not my daughter any more. You're becoming just like these English girls, hanging round the streets with men.'

'But I've been inside the house with Ama all the holidays. She knows I've been inside. I haven't been with a man.'

'I'm not talking about the holidays. I'm talking about when I trusted you and let you go off to school on your own, because your grandfather said I ought to let you go to school and there was no one to take you. You've been seen with a man.'

'Who? Who's seen me with a man?'

'Aysha! Don't talk to your father like that. Don't make him more angry.' Ama grabbed hold of Aysha's arm and pulled her to make her sit down, but Aysha stood up again.

'Who said I've been with a man? It's a lie.'

'Teachers don't tell lies,' Aba said. 'Your Mr Gilman has seen you. Your very nice art teacher. I met him today on my way home. He was good enough to

154

stop his car and speak to me about you – before it's too late. He is not a liar. He saw you every day from his car, on his way to school. And you were with a man. You can't deny it.'

'He's not my teacher. And he must be a liar. I've never been with a man.'

Aba picked up his plate and banged it down on the table again, so that rice flew all over the lace cloth.

'I don't care what you say. You're lying. But you won't get the chance to lie to me again or to run around with these English men. I'm sending you back to Jamdher. At least your honour will be safe there.'

'But who will look after Aysha? There's nobody there in Jamdher now her grandmother's gone. Will your brothers' wives look after her?' Aysha's mother laid her head on the table and cried again.

'She's almost a woman. It'll be time for her to marry soon. You'll have to go with her until she does marry. You can work in Piara's house, the two of you. Her husband's a rich man. He'll make sure nothing happens to you.'

'But I don't want to leave you,' Ama said.

'It doesn't matter what we want.' Aysha's father looked tired and brushed his long fringe out of his eyes. 'It's what's good for the family that matters. Everyone in the family wants Aysha to marry well. She can't stay here if she's going to spoil her chances of marriage and bring disgrace on the family.'

Aysha sat down. And when her father went out into the living-room she still sat there at the table, staring at the turquoise-painted wall. Her father had done the painting one weekend because Dada had said the house looked dull and dirty and he had gone out and bought one small pot of turquoise paint. But there was a damp patch behind the table, where a flower of mould was putting out green branches through the turquoise paint. Aysha stared at the flowers, the damp and the dirt, growing bigger as she watched it, invading their house and taking it over all the time they were working, trying to clean it and make it look nice.

She didn't want to go back to Bangladesh. Not like this. Too much had changed. Too much had happened. In one year everything had changed. She could never go back to the way things had been. All her life, she had slept on a tiny straw bed next to her mother, in a room next to her grandparent's room, where the walls were so thin that if she woke up in the night she could hear her grandfather's snoring, a lullaby to soothe her back to sleep. All her life, it seemed, she had run wild round their compound and through most of the village, swimming and climbing trees with her cousins who were nearly all boys. All her life she had been sure that she'd go to the High School and then train to be a secretary in Sylhet or even in Dhaka and she'd marry a good, kind man.

She had been sure that her grandfather would choose just the right man. She had been sure that all she had to do was tell her grandmother the man she wanted Dada to choose. That was the way things were done and all her life she had been certain that things would happen that way in her life as well. But too many things had changed.

Her language had been taken away from her. Teachers in her English schools had slapped her gently on the hand and said, 'Now, now, we speak English here. It's for your own good. You'll never learn English if you speak Bengali.' They had said that to her every time she found herself next to someone she could make friends with who spoke Bengali. Often, when there was nobody to talk to her in the playground, Aysha had played with words in her head, Bengali words and songs, all the songs she had ever heard her grandmother singing, like a tape recording going round and round in her head. For so many months she had longed to go back to Bangladesh, to go to a school where they spoke Bengali. But the worn out tape had got fainter and fainter and now she couldn't remember all of the words.

Once, when a teacher had told her to write something in her own words, she had looked puzzled and said, 'You mean in Bengali?' But that wasn't what the teacher had meant. The Bengali words weren't her own words any longer. They were only the words she could use at home.

But the words in English didn't belong to her, either. She made too many mistakes, used words in the wrong places so that people laughed at her. Slowly, slowly, she was having to make her own words, to remake her language, her very own language, out of the two languages that other people had thrown at her. She was remaking her own world. She could never go back to Bangladesh for good. She had two languages and she didn't quite belong in either of them. And she had two homes, both places where she didn't quite belong. Ama had been right. She wasn't the girl she used to be.

She stared and stared at the flowers of damp and

mould on the turquoise wall, and outside the kitchen window it slowly began to grow darker. Then she remembered Barry, the man she helped across the road because he was scared and always a little bit lost. She hadn't seen Barry for four weeks – not since the holidays had started, and she had stopped taking him across the road on her way to school. She wondered who was helping him across the road now. Perhaps she should have told someone, made sure that there was someone there to help him make his way to the Day Centre. She got up from the table.

Her father was in the living-room. She knew that without looking in there. So she went upstairs to her parents' bedroom. Ama was sitting on a chair next to the window, staring out at the street below. She had been crying a lot.

'I don't want to go back to Jamdher and leave your father again,' she said. 'We've been away from him for so long, I hardly know him. Aysha, why did you do this to us?'

Aysha stroked the rough, cool linoleum with her bare foot. It had been such a hot day. Then she sat down, cross-legged, on the floor beside her mother. 'I always thought you wanted to go back to Bangladesh. We've had a horrible time here. You said London was an evil place. I thought you wanted to go back.'

'I might have persuaded your father to let me work in the factory. Then I would have had friends here.'

'You've got Piara and all the other aunties back in Jamdher.'

Ama shook her head. 'You won't understand. I'm doing something different here. Something new, all by myself. Have we gone through all those terrible things here for nothing? Just to be sent back and be looked after by Piara's husband? I might have persuaded Aba to let me go and work in the factory. I might have done things I've never done before. But you won't understand. You're too young.'

Aysha was quiet. She understood what her mother was talking about, but she didn't know how to put it into words. It was the same thing she felt. She supposed they should both have been thinking about how bad it would be to leave Aba if he sent them back to Bangladesh. That would have been the right thing to think. But that wasn't what made them want to stay in England.

They both wanted to stay because England was a place where they had had to change, where they had become different people. It didn't even have to be England. Wherever they had moved to from Jamdher, they would have had to make different lives for themselves because things had to be different.

But they had landed up in England – in grey, dirty London, with Angela and her nan and Anwara and Darrell Foster and Doctor Choudhury and the Tamil men killed in the fire. Aysha was sure there were much nicer places in the world where they could have gone, but London was the first place where they had had to take charge of their own lives.

'You know that man, Ama? The man Aba was talking about.'

Ama turned round and Aysha stared past her at the dark cross of the window frame behind her head and beyond that the black lace pattern of the plane tree outside the window.

'I know now who it is that Mr Gilman was talking

about. It's a poor man who's like a child, even though he's older than Aba. I helped him across the road. Every day I helped him. He goes to the Day Centre near Angela's house, where all the people go who can't work outside. Someone looks after him there. But no one looks after him on his way to the Day Centre. So I did. I helped him across the road.'

'Aba said you were seen linking arms with him. You know we shouldn't do that, Aysha.'

'He held my arm. Like a little boy. He was lost and scared. I only took him across the road.'

'Why didn't you tell us?'

Aysha looked straight into her mother's eyes. 'I didn't think about it, Ama. That's what it's like in England. There is so much that's new here. I can't tell you everything. I didn't think it was bad to help him, Ama. He was so lost. And he can hardly say anything. He's deaf.'

Ama got up. 'I'll speak to your father. You go to bed now. Your Mr Gilman told Aba he wasn't taking good care of you, you know. That's what made him so angry. He said Mr Gilman told him he wasn't a good Muslim father. He told him he should go with you everywhere, so you don't go running around after men.'

'I'm glad he's not my teacher,' said Aysha. 'I don't know why he said that to Aba. Angela says he chases the girls. I'm scared of him. Everyone's afraid of him. He's a cruel man.' She placed her hands on her mother's shoulders.

'You're almost as tall as I am,' Ama said.

'I know.' Aysha stroked her own hand over the top

of her head to measure how tall she was and her fingers came to rest just above her mother's eyebrows.

'I'm going to speak to Aba,' Aysha said. 'You don't have to speak to him, Ama. I'll tell him. I'll tell him about Barry. And I'll tell him we don't want to go away from here. He'll listen to me.'

Chapter Sixteen

On the first day back at school after the summer holidays, there were hundreds of new first years wandering about. Aysha and Angela took charge of a class, going to meet them when the bells rang and showing them where to go for their next lesson. Aysha knew her way around the whole of the school. She could hardly remember what it felt like to be lost. And there were so many familiar faces now, so many teachers and pupils calling out to her.

'Hi, Aysha! Wotcha, Aysha! Have a good holiday, Aysha?' Aysha had an answer for all of them. It wasn't just that she knew everyone. She felt as if she had come home.

There were new teachers at the school as well, new teachers all doing the same as the old teachers. In the first lesson, they talked about what they had done in the holidays and then the class had to write about what they had done in the holidays. It didn't matter what subject lesson Aysha's class ended up in, they still had to write about what they had done in the holidays.

Only the new science teacher was different. 'Miss, please don't ask us to write about our holidays!' Angela said. 'I didn't do nothing!'

'Don't call out. I like people to put their hand up in my lesson.' She didn't tell them her name. 'We're going to talk about careers today. About what you want to be when you grow up.'

'That's not science, Miss. That's Careers. And we don't do Careers till we're fifteen.'

'Don't call out. Put your hands up if you've got anything to say. It's important to think about careers all the time. What about careers in science?'

'Miss, this is boring!'

'Yeh, Miss. When are we going to do some science?'

The new teacher sat down at the front, far away from them all. She glared at them and snarled, her scared eyes scanning the whole class, like a fox facing a pack of hounds. Aysha smiled at the teacher and whispered in Bengali, 'Oh, help!'

'We speak English in this school.' The new teacher's voice cracked and splintered, like a ruler breaking as it hits the desk. She tried again, speaking more quietly this time because the class was quiet. 'We speak English or we shut up. And we put our hands up when we want to speak.'

She went round the class, asking everyone, one by one, what they wanted to be when they grew up.

'Miss, I want to be an 'airdresser,' Angela smiled when the teacher finally brought her question back to the front bench where most of the girls were sitting.

'Well, you need to know some science for that as well, you know.' The new teacher smiled for the first time.

Then she looked at Aysha. She had just finished her training course and no one had told her what to say to a pupil who couldn't speak English. She didn't know which Asian language Aysha spoke, but it didn't really matter. The only language Miss Power had ever learned was French and she had dropped that when she was fourteen. Even if she hadn't done, it wouldn't have been any good to her. The whole class was silent. She had no idea what to say.

So she smiled and nodded at Aysha and went straight on to Emma who wanted to be a fashion model and Tracy, who wanted to be a beautician. Then she clapped her hands and called out, 'Anyone else? Have I missed anyone out? If not, can we get on and do some work now, please? That was just so I could get to know you a little bit.'

The boys at the back cheered. Someone called out, 'You can get to know me a lot, darling,' and then Aysha put her hand up.

The teacher ordered three of the boys to stand outside and two more shouted, 'Can I go too, Miss?' Then she lost her temper. 'Right! You're all in detention!' For the second time the class went deadly silent.

Aysha still had her hand up.

'What's your name?' When she finally spoke to Aysha, Miss Power spoke louder than she had done when she was trying to get the whole class to be quiet. She cut a space round each word as if she were using a fine pair of scissors to cut out a very delicate paper chain.

One of the few boys on the back bench who hadn't been sent out of the room squeaked, cutting the words as finely as his breaking voice would let him, 'My – name's – Aysha.'

Aysha laughed. 'Oh, shut up, Wesley!' She laughed again. 'Tell them, Miss! They keep taking the mickey! You didn't ask me what I want to be, Miss.'

The door opened. Aysha put her hands over her eyes and peeped through her fingers. She knew the boys wouldn't stay outside their classroom for long, whoever put them there. But it wasn't the boys this time, storming back into the room. The headmistress opened the door a crack and called Miss Power outside. The class sat and giggled and whispered.

'Hey! Aysha! She thinks you can't speak English,' Wesley said. 'She didn't know what to say to you. You ought to keep your mouth shut. You won't have to do no work if she thinks you can't speak English.'

'But I can,' said Aysha. 'And I'm going to tell her.'

'You must be mad.'

'I'll get you, Wesley Briggs! Aysha's not as mad as you are!' Angela was just about to storm to the back of the class when the door opened once again and the Head came in.

A girl walked in after her, very slowly, a girl from Bangladesh, in a bright green shalwar kameez and delicate gold sandals with high heels. Her name was Momtaz.

'I'm putting Momtaz in here,' the Head said, 'so Aysha can look after her.'

'She can sit in between us, Miss,' Angela shouted and then put her hand up and then dashed to the front of the class to get Momtaz. The Head went out of the room again to talk to Miss Power and the boys outside.

'Oh no!' Wesley lifted the lid of his desk and hid behind it and groaned. 'Not another foreigner!' Then he peeped over the top of the desk, grinning, and ducked down again as Angela threw her pencil case at him.

'I didn't mean it! Honest, Angela!'

Angela shot to the back of the class and smashed the desk lid down on his fingers.

'I didn't mean it, Momtaz.' Wesley blew on his fingers and tucked them under his armpits. 'You can come and sit next to me any time.'

Momtaz was shy and tiny and told Aysha she had never learned any English before. Angela said, 'I bet you're a good runner. Aysha's the best runner in the class and she's from Bangladesh.' Aysha translated and Momtaz laughed and shook her head. 'I hate running. I can't stand sport.'

Then Miss Power came back into the room. She sent the boys back to their seats and sat down at her desk again. 'Where were we?'

Aysha put her hand up.

'We were talking about what we all want to be. But you forgot to ask me my name, Miss. And now Momtaz is here. This is Momtaz and I don't know what she wants to be yet.' She grinned at the teacher. Wesley and the others would think she was big-headed, but she didn't care.

'My name's Aysha. And I'm going to be a doctor.'

MIRJAM PRESSLER

Shylock's Daughter

Venice, 1568

Jessica is sixteen – and trapped. She's tired of the endless rules of the Jewish Ghetto. Tired of her father Shylock's meanness. Now she wants to be free.

Lorenzo is everything Jessica ever wanted – handsome, charming, aristocratic and flattering. Jessica can't help but fall in love. After all, Lorenzo is surely her way into a wonderful new life.

But Lorenzo is a Christian and Jessica is a Jew. And the price of freedom can be desperately high . . .

'Extraordinarily powerful.' *Literary Review*

'An eye-opening and empathetic novel, with resonances for any society where racism exists and cultures clash.' Nicolette Jones, *Sunday Times*

MALORIE BLACKMAN

Tell Me No Lies

Mike could feel her eyes like lasers, boring into his back. He had to fight not to turn around. Did she know his face? Had she recognized him?

Gemma cuts out pictures for her scrapbooks – pictures of mothers, like the one she will never, ever see again.

Mike is a new boy at school – a boy who is desperate not to be noticed. Who has a secret so terrible it will haunt him for ever.

But Gemma's sure she's seen Mike's face before. And now she's out to get him . . .

'Pacy, hard-hitting . . . a brave novel about true courage.' Lindsey Fraser, Scottish Book Trust